Path to Nowhere

A Shady Acres Mystery, Book 2

By Cynthia Hickey

To all Shelby's fans!

1

Three weeks without a murder had me walking with a definite spring in my step. "Good morning!" I sang to everyone I passed on my way to breakfast.

"Shelby Hart!" Alice Johnson, manager of Shady Acres, narrowed her eyes. "What are you wearing?"

"Shorts and a blouse." I glanced down at my favorite rainboots, black and white striped with a red bow on the back, a light blue blouse and cut off denims. Was something wrong with her eyes?

"Untie the blouse at your waist. Your stomach is showing. You'll give the old men a heart attack."

"But, it's hot today." I did as instructed...she was my boss after all. Now, my shirt was wrinkled where I'd tied it. I sighed. "Do you have a certain chore for me today?" As the community gardener and event coordinator, I had learned not to plan my to-do list before speaking with Alice.

"That old brick path needs cleaned up."

"Where does it go?"

"Nowhere...I don't care. It's an eye sore. Now that we're under new management, I'll be hiring an interior decorator to redo the cottages. We're going to make this the ritzy place for retirees that it was meant to be." Without a dismissal, she turned and headed for the main building.

I shrugged. We could have at least walked together.

"Bossy, witch."

Startled, I turned, knocking a stack of magazines from the hands of our receptionist Teresa Givens. "Me?"

"Of course not. Alice." She stooped to pick up the magazines.

I stopped to help, glancing at the headshot of one of Hollywood's hunks. "I didn't know you read these."

She shrugged. "I'm fascinated by the lives of the rich and famous. When I was little, I dreamed of being a movie star. I want a big house, a fancy car, and a man who showers me with gifts."

"You've got the looks for it." I stood and handed her the ones I'd gathered. "What's stopping you?"

"Money, mostly. Thanks." She wrapped her arms around the pile and turned toward the cottages. "See you at breakfast. Alice was insistent I put these away so clients wouldn't see my 'trashy' magazines. Her words, not mine."

How well I understood. Every

employee at Shady Acres had received a tongue lashing from Alice at one time or another. It was worse after the murders last month. Now, Alice seemed to think herself invincible.

She'd been the primary target until I stuck my nose where it didn't belong. Then, the target had switched to me.

I pushed open the double doors to the dining hall. Conversation, laughter, and the clink of eating utensils against dishes assaulted my ears. Taking a deep breath, I glanced around for Grandma and Heath.

Grandma sat at a table with Harold Ball, Marvin Hall, William Jamison, and Bob Satchett. Of course, she was the only female at the table.

My eyes widened at the fluorescent pink jogging suit she wore with royal blue heels. Shaking my head, I moved to the employee table where Heath was already digging into a mountain of pancakes.

"Hello, gorgeous." He swallowed and grinned.

I planted a quick kiss on his cheek. "Good morning." I headed for the buffet and filled my plate with fruit, cheese, and a croissant before sitting next to Heath.

"Did Alice tell you about her plans for the place?"

"Redecorating? Yep." I bit into a strawberry. "I like my cottage just fine. What's on the agenda for you?"

"I need to look into Dave's and Harry's cottages and see what repairs, if any, need to be made." His tone sobered as he mentioned the deceased Dave, and his killer Harry. "Alice wants those cabins done first. She said she already has people interested in renting them."

"She wants me to clear some path to nowhere." I buttered my croissant. "Which is fine. I have a lot of the grounds looking pretty good, other than a few bushes that need trimming, I could do with a large project." Not to mention I needed to come up with a social activity for that weekend.

"Well, we need to earn our keep, I suppose."

I shrugged. At least she had stopped giving me portions of her own job to do. For a while, I had been lucky to get any of my own work done, as Alice tended to treat me as her personal assistant. It was still better than a room full of rowdy third graders, which is what I worked at before. I finished off my breakfast and grabbed Heath's plate and mine. "I'll set these on the counter on my way out. I might as well get a look at this path."

I waved at Grandma on my way out and headed for the part of the grounds I had yet to get to. I hadn't counted it a priority since it was at the back. Shouldn't I first work on what could be seen? Still, orders were orders.

After stopping at my cottage for a

floppy straw hat to ward off the summer's hot sun, I made my way to the bleached blond brick walkway, my mind already deciding the types of colorful foliage I would line it with. Flowers for spring and summer, evergreens for fall and winter.

Weeds and grass grew between the bricks. First priority would be grass and weed killer. I continued along my brick road until I came to a nine foot overgrown hedge hidden by a stand of trees.

I glanced right, then left. The hedge stretched as far as I could see. How had I missed something so large? Maybe because I'd been busy solving a couple of murders and trying to stay alive myself. I shoved aside branches and followed the hedge until I located a rusty gate. I pushed it open, wincing at the loud shriek the hinges made.

A maze! One that needed work, but a

maze nevertheless. I'd found my next social event. How fun to traverse the maze at night by flashlight. I'd have to work fast to have it ready by the weekend, but a backhoe would rake up the fallen leaves quick enough. It would take a while to trim the hedges, but that wouldn't stop the community from having a bit of fun. The prize would be at the end.

Deciding I needed something to show my way so I wouldn't get lost, I headed back to my cottage for some ribbon leftover from a project I'd done with my students once upon a time.

Armed with red ribbon and a pair of scissors, I hurried back and left a bow at each intersection, removing the ribbon when I realized I'd gone the wrong way. Oh, this was fun! I could already imagine the hilarity that would ensue when it was dark.

After an hour of traversing the very

difficult trails, I wished for a drink of water. Why hadn't I filled my cooler and brought the wheelbarrow? I sat on a stone bench and fanned by face with my hat.

The maze was very peaceful. Birds twittered from within and from somewhere came the sound of trickling water. It would be beautiful when finished.

Rested, I pushed to my feet and continued on my personal treasure hunt. There had to be an end to the thing. I only hoped it didn't come back out before revealing something wonderful. A place I could set the prize for the participant who got there first.

I rounded a corner. Oh, a gazebo! It needed paint, and one of the benches sagged, but it was the perfect place to hide a...body?

Sensible navy pumps covering feet connected to shapely calves, hung down the gazebo steps. I dashed forward, pulling my phone from my pocket as I ran.

Teresa Givens, a knife protruding from her chest, stared up at me with dead eyes.

I dialed Officer Ted Lawrence, who also happened to be Grandma's boyfriend. "This is Shelby. I found a dead body."

"Who?"

"This isn't the time for teasing! Teresa Givens is lying in the gazebo in the maze with a knife in her chest."

He sighed. "I'm on my way."

"Oh, Ted?"

"Yeah?"

"Follow the brick road, then the hedge, then the red bows, and...oh, bring me some water, please. I'm dying here." I cringed at my choice of words.

He said a few colorful expletives and hung up.

I dialed Alice next. "Teresa is dead in the maze."

"Excuse me?"

"Dead as in stabbed in the chest."

"We have a maze?"

"Alice!"

"Sorry, I wasn't aware."

I gave her the same directions I had given Officer Ted, then dialed Heath. "Teresa is dead in the maze." I should have recorded my first conversation and replayed it to all interested parties.

"Are you okay?"

Finally, someone cared about me and the victim. "I'm fine." Tears burned my eyes. "But Teresa isn't. Oh, Heath, all she wanted was to be a movie star." I plopped onto the sagging bench across from the body. "Who would want to kill such a nice girl?"

"I'm on my way. Oh, there's Alice. I'll come with her." Click.

Great. The one woman other than me

who had a crush on Heath would now get to follow the maze with him.

Doing my best not to look at Teresa's body, I decided to stay busy seeing what all needed done to get the gazebo in shape. Maybe I could ask Heath to fit it into his schedule to help. I had an engraved wooden box given to me by my lousy, coward of an ex-fiance that would make the perfect prize. I would set it right on the banister.

Where was everybody? I resumed my seat and fanning my face. It had taken me a long time to get here, but I left them a clear path.

An hour after I called Officer Ted, he arrived on the scene with Grandma, Alice, and Heath in tow. Grandma stood over the body, a hungry gleam in her eye. Since the first murders, she fancied herself a sleuth and seemed to look for mysteries every day.

"I don't think she was killed here," I

said.

Officer Ted glanced my way. "Why do you say that?"

"There's no pool of blood under her." I stood. "Now, I'm not saying she wasn't killed in the maze, that's possible, but I'm right, aren't I?"

"Most likely." He didn't look the least bit happy about my observation. "Stay out of it, Shelby."

"I didn't have anything else to do while waiting on y'all, but think about it."

"Your job here is done."

"Not really. I have a lot of work to do before the weekend haunted maze activity—"

"What a great idea!" Grandma clapped her hands. "It'll be even more scary now that someone was killed."

Officer Ted scowled. "This is a crime scene. I doubt it's cleared in time for you to prepare for this weekend."

Of course, he was right. I needed

another plan, and I was fresh out of ideas. No, wait. I'd play off the scariness of this and build people's anticipation with a murder mystery dinner in the dining hall.

I skirted Teresa's body, tears springing fresh. I really thought we could have become friends, given the time, if not for the fact the girl was very secretive about what she did after work. I glanced one more time at her, then squatted next to her.

"Did you see this?" I pointed to the bouquet of roses under her. "I think she was here with a beau."

2

"She wasn't killed here," Officer said.

"No, but the killer let her keep the flowers." To me, that signified someone she knew, possibly someone who cared for her in a sick twisted way.

Two detectives arrived, followed by two other men in uniform. They immediately strung yellow crime scene tape, blocking off the gazebo area and shooing us to the other side of the tape.

"The rest of you can leave. Shelby stay here, I have questions for you." Officer Ted gave me a stern look, then turned to converse with one of the other officers.

"I'm not going anywhere," Grandma said. She pulled a granola bar and a bottle of water from her cavernous purse. "Here, you look peaked."

"Bless you." I drank half the bottle in one go. "I've been out here for a long time."

Heath pulled me into a hug. "I'm so sorry you had to be the one to find her."

"Seems to be my lot in life at Shady Acres." Gracious, I hoped not. While solving mysteries was fun, I hated that people died. Why couldn't it be something as simple as a stolen ring? That would still give Grandma and I the thrill of the hunt without someone losing their life. Tears welled again.

I couldn't remember crying as much in my entire life as I had in the last month of working at Shady Acres. "This place is cursed."

Heath chuckled. "No, you're just unlucky."

I peered up at his face. "This is my fault?"

"I didn't mean it that way. I only meant that you have poor luck in being the one to stumble across the bodies." He kissed the tip of my nose. "I'm sorry."

I nodded. He was right, but it was because I traversed the entire grounds doing my job. Most of the residents didn't follow the same paths I did.

After another hour and my second water bottle, I had a whole different body function problem. For one of the few times since meeting Officer Ted, I looked up with anticipation as he came to question me. Soon, I could go home to my humble cottage.

"Start from the beginning." Officer Ted pulled a pen and small notepad from his pocket.

"Well, Alice told me to clean up this

path. I followed it and found this maze. Then, to keep from getting lost, I—"

He rolled his eyes. "Can you skip to the part about finding the victim?"

I sighed. "Fine. I thought it might be fun to do a community event in the maze and was searching for a place to leave the prize. I found the gazebo...and Teresa. I didn't touch her." I crossed my arms and glared.

"So, you don't know whether she was alive when you got here?"

"I'm pretty sure she wasn't. Her chest wasn't moving and she wasn't blinking. Last time I found a body, you yelled at me for touching...it. I wasn't going to make that mistake again." Please God, don't have let her have been alive when I arrived and I didn't do anything to help.

He shook his head. "Then..."

"I called you, then Alice, then Heath."

He snapped his notebook closed. "We're finished for now. You may go."

He turned in a definite move of dismissal.

Heath put an arm around my shoulders and we followed my path of red bows out of the maze and back to my cottage. Alice was the only one who stayed behind, most likely doing what she thought was her managerial duties.

"Good morning!"

I opened the door to see Mom on my sofa, a cup of tea in her hand. "Mom?"

"I've made tea." She held up her cup. "There's plenty."

"What are you doing here?"

"I'm staying with your grandmother while my house is being fumigated."

"You are?" Grandma frowned. "You know how I feel about you cramping my style."

"You'll get over it. You're an old woman. I won't cramp my daughter's style."

I had no idea what style they were talking about. I plopped on the sofa next to her and explained about my morning.

"Oh, dear, you do have a way with murder, don't you?"

"What?" I frowned.

"This is what...the third body you've found? You've a gift, dear, and while I don't condone you putting yourself in danger, you should use this gift and find out who killed the poor girl."

"I think I'll stay out of this one." I shuddered.

"What if someone else dies because you didn't snoop around?"

Grandma patted me on the hand. "I'll help you."

Good grief. I glanced at Heath for help.

He shrugged. "This is between the three of you...and the police. Ted will have a heart attack if you get involved, so keep that in mind."

"I can handle Ted," Grandma said. "All he needs is a little female persuasion and he's putty in my hands."

Gross. "I don't plan on getting involved."

"You won't be able to help yourself," Grandma said. "It's a sickness."

"The cure is minding my own business." I moved to the kitchen and poured myself a cup of tea. My family was going to pull me into this murder whether I liked it or not. Don't they remember that me and Cheryl, my best friend, were almost burned alive by the last killer?

Deciding I needed a rational person to talk to, I headed for my room and called Cheryl. I told her what had happened and settled back against the bed pillows to listen while she reassured me that everything would be okay.

"Another one?"

"I don't ask for these things to happen, Cheryl."

"If I wasn't teaching summer school,

I'd come out and help you solve the crime."

"I'm not getting involved."

Her loud laughter showed she didn't believe me. "Sure."

"I'm serious."

"You won't be able to help yourself. You'll hear or see something and off you'll go. I'm only sorry I'll miss it."

"You actually enjoyed almost being killed?"

"Well, not that part, but the rest was entertaining."

I was surrounded by insane people. "I hoped you'd be the voice of reason."

"Sorry. All reason was lost a long time ago. Look, I've got to go grade a ton of paperwork. Keep me posted. Ciao!" Click.

"Here." Grandma entered the room and dumped her bag on the bed next to me. "I bought you a Tazor, a tiny flashlight, and some pepper spray. I figured after what happened before you would need them. How right I am. I'll buy you a gun if you want one. I ordered me a hot pink number that's to die for."

I cringed at her choice of words. "I don't want a gun." But, I did accept the other things. Contrary to my own resolve, I knew everyone was right and I'd be dragged into trying to find out who killed Teresa.

"So, what's first?" She sat next to me.

"I'm planning a murder mystery dinner for Saturday night. I need to make the fliers, figure out the crime—"

"A woman gets stabbed in the chest."

"Grandma, please."

She held up a hand. "Hear me out. If the victim dies," she made finger quotes, "the same way as poor Teresa, the killer, who will most likely be at the party, might slip up and betray themselves."

She made a good point. "What makes you think the killer is a resident?"

"It's always someone close." She

patted my knee. "Remember, I'm an expert because of all the crime shows on TV."

No matter what I said, I couldn't convince her that those were so often fabricated as to be very far from the truth. I nibbled my bottom lip. "I suppose...I'll be the victim. Everyone who attends will draw a slip of paper. On one of them will be an X. That person will be the killer, and I'll give them the background information on the murder. It will be up to everyone else to mingle and ask questions to find out who the person with the X is. It just might work. But..." I held up my hand to ward off her protests..."I won't die the same way. That would be disrespectful."

"Of course your plan will work. You have my brain after all."

Heaven help me.

A glance at the clock told me lunch was being served. Despite the rough morning, my stomach rumbled. A granola bar didn't tide over a person with a high metabolism for very long. Maybe, the conversation in the dining hall would center around Teresa and I'd hear something informative.

The four of us entered the dining hall and all heads turned in our direction. After a couple of intensely quiet seconds, the murmuring started.

Birdie Sorenson, her haired died lavender this month, approached at a fast clip. "You going to help Teresa like you helped Maybelle?"

"I didn't help Maybelle. I found her dead." I headed for my table.

"But, you found her killer, just as I asked."

"Her killer found me is more accurate."

"Stop dancing around the question. Are you going to investigate or not?"

I detested lying, but found it the wiser

course of action in this case. "Not." I grabbed a plate and headed for the buffet.

Like a sparrow chasing bird crumbs, she followed. "Why not?"

"I prefer living, thank you." I grabbed a ham and cheese croissant sandwich and a small prepared salad. "Please don't make up the fabrication that I'm going to snoop, all right?"

She crossed her skinny arms. "I never figured you for a coward."

I rolled my eyes and sighed. "Wanting to live is not being a coward." I carried my plate back to the table and took my seat.

"She's tenacious," Heath said.

"That's one word for her."

He gave me a quick one-armed hug. "Chin up. No one can make you do what you don't want to."

True, but I tended to want to make my friends and family happy. Which caused me to do things I didn't want to do.

"What do you think about me digging into Teresa's death?"

"It scares the dickens out of me. You had a very close call the last time."

Too close. "Grandma bought me a Tazor."

"Well, that's something."

I bit into my croissant and studied those in the room. Just the usual faces. Not one person looked like a killer or that they would have been interested in a romantic relationship with Teresa. If...my deduction about the roses was correct. The men in the room were in their sixties. Teresa couldn't have been over twenty-five.

The murder mystery party might be fun, but I doubted it would lead me to her killer. "I don't think her killer was a resident."

"Why do you say that?"

"I still think the roses were from an admirer. Can you see someone as pretty as Teresa with one of these elderly men?"

"No, but that doesn't mean they didn't want to see themselves with her."

3

*H*eath was right. Age had no limit. I looked around the room with new eyes, and found no further information. I still couldn't picture any of them as Teresa's killer.

"Hello, Heath."

We both turned. Standing next to our table, dressed in a stylish grey suit with a vibrant scarlet blouse, was a raven haired woman with eyes as dark as night. I'd never seen anyone more beautiful.

"Lauren!" Heath bolted to his feet, spilling his glass of tea across the white tablecloth. "What are you doing here?"

"I'm the interior decorator, silly." She fiddled with the collar of his tee shirt. "Aren't you happy to see me?"

He cast a suspiciously guilty look at me, then grabbed her arm and dragged her to a far corner of the room. Forget the mystery of Teresa's death. I wanted to know who Ms. Gorgeous was and how she knew the man I thought was my boyfriend.

Either way, Heath did not look happy to see her, and, considering the many furtive glances in my direction, didn't want me to know about her. After sopping up the spilled tea and rolling the tablecloth into a ball, I carried my half-full plate out the door and to my cottage. Let them resolve their issues in peace. But, guaranteed I'd be getting some answers soon.

I veered before reaching my cottage and headed for the tables poolside. After removing my garden boots, I hung my feet in the cool water, ate my lunch, and tried not to think about what was transpiring between Heath and the beauty queen.

"Why aren't you working?"

I glanced over my shoulder to spot Alice glaring at me. What else was new? "Lunch."

She took a quick look at her watch. "Very well. Not too much longer. I want you to meet the interior decorator."

"Why? We won't be working together."

"Because you're my Jill of all trades. You might be working with her."

Gag. "What happened in the maze after we left?"

She set her ever-present clipboard on a table. "They found where she was murdered. At least, they found a blood soaked patch of ground just inside the entrance. I'm surprised you didn't see it. Your boot print was smack in the middle of it. Officer Lawrence was not happy about that, I can tell you."

Gross. I lifted my boots. Sure enough, in the tred of my right boot, was reddish brown mud. I almost washed it off right then and there in the pool, but figured it was evidence. I'd turn it over as long as I got a promise my favorite boots would be returned.

"The decorator is in the dining hall talking to Heath," I said, setting my boots at arm's length from me.

"Oh, good. I'm sure she will have a lot of things for him to do."

No doubt. I sighed and pushed to my feet. "Where's Officer Ted now?"

She shrugged. "Probably at your cottage."

"Return this for me, will you?" I thrust my plate into her hands and without waiting for an answer, picked up my boots and ran across the hot path to home.

Officer Ted leaned against the outside wall, waiting for me. "You must have spoken with Alice."

"Yes. I want these back." I handed over the boots.

"Just as soon as the forensics team is finished with them."

Does this make me a suspect?" I had been one with the first murder, and didn't relish a repeat.

"Should you be?"

"Don't toy with me or I'll sic Grandma on you."

He chuckled. "No, you're not a suspect. We only want what's on your boot." He gave me a jaunty salute and sauntered away.

I unlocked my cottage door, chose a pair of bright blue boots with hot pink polka dots and headed for my toolshed. Getting a start on spraying weed and grass killer on the brick path shouldn't destroy evidence since the crime took place within the walls of the maze. I could clear the path and start work on trimming the overgrown bushes and plant some flowers. All of which would take me most of the week.

If I stayed busy, and away from the others, perhaps there wouldn't be any more pressure to investigate. No such luck. Grandma stood outside the tool shed waiting for me with arms crossed.

"What are you doing?" She asked.

"Working." I unlocked the padlock and slid the doors open.

"Why aren't you investigating?"

"Shady Acres doesn't pay me to investigate. They pay me to work. Besides, I thought the party on Saturday would be the best time to start snooping." I stepped into the dark shed and stretched to remove the bottle of vegetation killer from the top shelf. Armed with it and the sprayer, I loaded them into the wheelbarrow and exited, locking the door behind me.

"I'm working on the path leading to the maze. Feel free to come along and snoop."

"Oh, goody. Maybe I'll find a strand of hair or something. I've a magnifying glass and tweezers in my bag."

Of course she did. I wheeled my supplies to the front of the path, pausing only once to wipe the perspiration from my brow. It was going to be a scorching afternoon.

"Here." Grandma plopped a floppy pink hat on my head. "You don't want to freckle."

"Thank you. I left my hat in the gazebo."

After half an hour, Grandma marched up the walkway. "I can't find anything out here. How much trouble do you think I'll get into if I go past the yellow tape?"

"A lot. It's against the law." I blinked against the sweat dripping into my eyes.

Maybe I should do the hard work in the cooler mornings and work on community activities during the heat of the day.

"I'm finished for now." I loaded my things into the wheelbarrow.

"Who is that with Alice?" Grandma pointed.

I glanced up to see Alice, Lauren, and Heath strolling toward us. The only one smiling was Lauren. I glanced at my dirt smeared arms and legs, a stain on my blouse, and blew hair out of my eyes. Wonderful.

"Shelby, this is our decorator, Lauren." Alice took a deep breath through her nose. "Heath's fiancée." That explained Alice's sour expression. She had a crush on Heath that had now been crushed under Lauren's stiletto.

"Ex-fiancee." Heath's eyes implored me not to freak out.

"Darling." Lauren turned to him. "I said I was sorry."

He exhaled sharply, then mouthed the words, "We'll talk later," to me.

I gave a small nod to let him know I understood. "It's nice to meet you. Forgive me for not shaking your hand, Lauren, but as you can see I've been working."

"That's fine. I love playing in the dirt myself from time-to-time." She smiled, revealing perfect straight and white teeth.

"I've told Lauren that if she needs any help, to call on you and Heath. I'm sure you won't mind." Alice turned and marched away.

Lauren continued to smile. "Wonderful. I'd like to set a meeting for…" she glanced at a gold watch on her delicate wrist. "one hour. That should give you time to clean up, Shelby. I'm staying in the main building, room number three. See you then." If her hips swayed any harder as she walked away, she was going to break something.

"Shelby—"

"Talk to me on the way to the tool shed. Grandma, go home. This is my business."

"Oh, pooh. You're as bad as your mother."

"We aren't engaged, Shelby, no matter what Lauren says."

"She seems a bit confused, then." I unlocked the padlock on the shed and rolled the wheelbarrow inside.

"I caught her with another man. No amount of apologies can erase that." He gripped my shoulders and turned me to face him.

"We don't have an...exclusive relationship, Heath. It's really none of my business."

"I thought we were an item." Pain flickered across his bluebonnet eyes.

"Are we? I think the return of Lauren might put a kink in that." I swallowed against the mound growing in my throat.

"It doesn't. I promise." He took my hand. "I'll walk you to your cottage."

I tried to push aside my suspicions, but after being ditched at the altar, and the groom-to-be replacing me within the week, I found it hard to trust the words coming from Heath's mouth. I kept my hand in his, but kept my gaze straight ahead. My heart needed to be guarded until things were clearer.

Back at the cottage, while Heath waited in the living room, I scanned my closet for something to wear that wouldn't make me pale too much in comparison with Lauren. I chose a pair of strappy sandals and a sundress that fit at the bodice and flared away at the waist. After a quick shower, I smoothed back my unruly mass of curls and secured them with a barrett. After a quick dab of mascara and lipgloss, I was as good as I could get.

"You look nice." Heath took my hand again. "Don't let Lauren intimidate you."

I blinked up at him. Did I look as if I'd be intimidated? Maybe I should change. His firm grip on my hand, kept me at his side.

"You are beautiful, Shelby. Inside and out." He led me out the door and up the stairs of the main building to room three.

He rapped his knuckles three times, then stepped back for her to open the door. Great. She had changed into skinny jeans and a tee shirt. Now, I was overdressed. I had the feeling I couldn't win with this woman.

"You clean up nice, Shelby." She stepped back and ushered us in. "Have a seat."

The round table in one corner of the room had three chairs and several sheets of paper waiting for us. Heath pulled out my chair and sat down until Lauren cleared her throat. Rolling his eyes, he stood and did the same for her.

I hid a smirk. Usually the gentleman, his not pulling out her chair until asked spoke volumes about his feelings. I glanced at the page in front of me. It seemed as if I were to be Lauren's personal assistant while she was here.

"I can't do all this and my job, too." I slid the paper across the table.

"Alice assured me you would have time." Lauren crossed her arms, her smile never fading. "She said you were a marvel at time management. Don't sell yourself short, Shelby. That's no way to get ahead in this world."

"I'm perfectly happy where I am. Not only am I the only gardener here, but I plan the weekly social events. I can give you one hour a day and no more."

She sighed dramatically. "It will have to do. I'll just have to impose more on Heath."

Wait a minute. I needed to rethink

things here. "I'll try to give you more, but no promises." The least amount of time she spent alone with Heath, the less temptation put in front of him.

He glanced from her to me. "Don't I get a say in this? I have work, too."

Lauren tilted her head. "You're the handyman, darling. This is handyman work."

"You make my job sound beneath you."

"Not at all. You're very good with your hands." She winked at me.

I scowled and focused on my list of chores, wanting nothing more than to shove the paper down her pretty throat.

"Although, it is a mystery as to why you quit working for Daddy and...came here."

Ah, there was more to Heath's background than he's told me.

"I didn't think it wise to continue working there after breaking off our engagement. Besides, I'm not the desk type of guy. I like working outside. Shady Acres is perfect for me."

"Give me a week." She trailed a manicured fingernail down his arm. "I'll change your mind."

He stood suddenly enough to knock his chair over. "Let's go, Shelby. We know what's expected of us."

"See you two in the morning directly after breakfast," her voice trilled after us.

"I should have left the state," Heath said the moment the door closed behind us. "But then, I wouldn't have met you." He smiled down at me.

My heart did a somersault. "I don't think she's going to make things pleasant for us."

"If I could keep Alice at arm's length, I can do the same with Lauren."

I didn't think so, but held my tongue. Only time would tell whether I had a boyfriend at the end of the week.

4

Alice seemed to have the same thing on her mind as I did. By the weekend, Heath had spent very little time alone with Lauren. Instead, Alice kept Lauren locked in her office with her going over plans for the cottages.

As for plans, I had my own to finalize with the murder mystery dinner that evening. I knocked twice on Alice's office door and waited for her to answer.

"I'm busy." Alice opened the door, spit out the words, and started to close it.

I shoved my foot in the opening. "I need to finish the plans for this evening."

"Very well." She opened the door wider.

Lauren and two men I had yet to meet sat across from Alice's desk. Both in their fifties, both very handsome. If they were new residents, the women were going to be all a flutter competing for their attention.

"Shelby, this is Alan Barker and Damon Markson. They'll be moving into the vacated cottages. Lauren will renovate their places first."

"Welcome." I handed them both a flier for that evening's events. "I hope you can join us."

"Is that the flier I need to approve?" Alice frowned.

"Yes. But, since we haven't been able to get together, I handed them out three days ago." Hopefully, she was okay with the information.

She glanced over the paper. "It looks fine. Next time, I need to see them before they're handed out."

The two men watched our exchange with curiosity. Then, they stood, shook my hand, and left the room, promising to be at the party.

"When are they moving in?" I cut a sideways glance at Lauren, relieved to see her engrossed in sketches on the desk.

"Tonight. We'll decorate around them to the best of our ability," Alice said. "They both seem to be in a hurry. Oh, Lauren is having a delivery of paint delivered any minute. Could you go to the front entrance and wait?"

"Sure." I only had like a million things to do. Dismissed, I left without speaking a word to Lauren or her to me. Strange, since I tended to speak with everyone I came across.

Making my way around the main building, I took a seat on a cement bench out front and waited for the delivery. I glanced at my watch. I should have asked when the delivery was scheduled, I suppose. It wasn't like I had time to waste.

There were decorations to hang, paper pieces to cut and mark one with an X, the background info for the killer to be printed...my to-do list seemed never ending.

Finally. A white van pulled into the parking lot. I got to my feet as a young man with a sad expression climbed out. He loaded can after can of paint onto a dolly, then rolled it toward me.

"Where would you like these?"

Oh, Alice hadn't said. "Just inside the door, I guess." Since we had yet to hire a new receptionist, all calls being forwarded to Alice, it should be all right to clutter the foyer temporarily.

He nodded and rolled the paint inside. I followed to find him staring at Teresa's name plate.

"Did you know her?" I asked.

"We've been dating for six months." He swiped the back of his hand across his face. "Do you mind if I take the nameplate."

"Go ahead. What's your name?"

"Scott Cline. I'd make my deliveries and take her to lunch." His words caught on a hiccup. "I sure will miss her."

"I'm sorry for your loss."

"Yeah, it's going to be especially hard since I've been hired on to help while the renovations are going on."

Really? Huh. I wondered whether Heath knew. "Well, welcome aboard." I thrust a flier at him. "I hope you can come. I've work to do, so I'll leave you to the unloading. Is there something I need to sign?" If he was going to be working there, I didn't think I needed to supervise him.

I signed the clipboard and set off to my cottage at a fast clip. I opened my door to see Mom and Grandma enjoying tea without me. "Gee, it's nice to know y'all feel comfortable enough to make yourselves at home."

"Guess what?" Mom grinned.

"I'm too busy to guess." I moved my laptop from the coffee table and the danger of spilled tea to the safety of the kitchen table.

"I'm going to work as receptionist until they hire someone."

"That's great. I just signed for a delivery for you." I booted up my laptop.

Mom bolted to her feet. "He's early!" She dashed outside, to her new job presumably.

"You should be more happy for her," Grandma said. "She needs something to fill her days."

"I am happy for her. I'm sorry I didn't have any balloons to release." I printed off the background info for the killer, then realized I had no way of getting the pages to the pretend murderer without everyone seeing. Darn. I would have to cheat and make Heath the bad guy. "I'm headed out again. Lock up when you leave."

"Would you like me to start on the decorations? I can help, you know."

"That would be wonderful. The supplies are already in the dining hall." I handed her a drawing of where I wanted everything. "The theme is twenties gangster."

"Wonderful! I'll wear my flapper dress again. I have one for you, too."

"I'll be dead and wearing all black."

"Oh, pooh, how melodramatic." She flitted from the cottage, leaving me to lock the door.

I located Heath replacing a lock on one of the vacant cottages. "I need you to be the killer tonight." I handed him his instructions.

"Okay. I thought you were going to

have a drawing."

I explained my reasoning, then smiled. "You get to kill me. Well, not really, and off screen, but you know..."

He chuckled and, folding the paper, stuck it in his back pocket. "You'll be the prettiest victim there." He planted a quick kiss on my cheek. "See you tonight."

"Did you know you had a helper hired? He's, was, Teresa's boyfriend."

"I heard I had someone starting in the morning, but didn't know it was Scott."

"You know him?"

"Yeah, he seems like a good kid. A hard worker, at least."

I hoped the poor guy didn't follow the same fate as Heath's previous helper. "See you tonight." I quick walked to the dining hall.

"Grandma, that is not what I told you to do." She had strung silver glittery streamers everywhere.

"I thought it would be nice to have a nighttime fantasy type of thing. I have sparkly stars to hang, too."

I shoved a streamer out of my face. "You can't walk in here if you hang all of those up. Take them down. The stars are okay."

"You ruin all my creativity." She started yanking down streamers, leaving swatches of tape on the ceiling tiles.

"How did you get them up there?"

She pointed to a ladder leaning against the wall. "How do you think?"

"You're too old to use a ladder."

She gave me a go-to-Hades look and stomped away.

"This is tacky." Lauren entered the room.

"I'm sorry we don't all have a degree in decorating." I wadded up dropped streamers and shoved them in the nearest garbage can.

"Oh, I don't have a degree. I'm just

good at what I do." She gave a coy smile and sashayed, yes sashayed, away.

I wanted to slap the smug look from her face. Instead, I started putting navy tablecloths on the tables, a record player with old tyme band music records stacked close by, and set a list of guidelines at each place setting. Finished, I stepped back to survey my work. Grandma's stars did lend a festive air to the room. With candles the only lighting for the evening, there would also be an air of mystery surrounding everything.

"This looks wonderful." Alice clasped her hands in front of her.

I gasped. "You scared me."

"Sorry." She fell into a chair. "I'm exhausted. That woman wears me out with her demands."

"Lauren?"

She nodded. "What does Heath see in her?"

"Uh, nothing?"

"We'd like to think that, wouldn't we? But...she's simpering and batting her eyelashes at him as we speak. The man is eating it up."

I glanced at the door, wanting nothing more than to go interrupt them. "He said it's over between them."

"Someone needs to tell her that." She exhaled sharply. "I'd better go get ready for the party. Maybe I'll set my hat for one of the new residents. They may be twenty years older, but they're both loaded. I have no idea why they've chosen such a simple place as Shady Acres to live."

"It will rival any retire community once we're finished updating." I took offense at her statement. I worked hard to get the grounds in order. "If I had help—"

"You do fine on your own. See you later." She wobbled, er, uh, marched, on wobbly stilettos. Some people were not meant to wear heels.

A quick glance at the wall clock had me sprinting for my cottage and the shower. Hanging on my bedroom door was a black flapper dress and a headband with a black feather. Grandma was determined to have her way somehow. Still, it beat the black leggings and baggy tee shirt I had planned on wearing.

Since I refused to cut my hair, I tried taming it with a straightener to no avail. I'd be a flapper with frizzy curls around my head. Sighing, I slipped my feet into strappy sandals and left the cottage.

On the flagstone pathway, I glanced in one direction, then in another as the dinner gong sounded. As if they were one body, cottage doors opened and residents filed out in 1920s splendor.

Heath came my way and slid his arms around my waist. "It looks as if you've come up with a winner idea again."

I stepped free of his hold. "From Lauren's arms to mine?"

He frowned. "I'm confused."

"Alice saw you all lovey-dovey with Lauren earlier."

"I told you it's all her." He reached for me again.

I took a step back. "I can't...not until you put her in her place."

He ran his fingers through his hair, making the strands stand on end like stalks of wheat. "I need you to trust me, Shelby."

"I'm trying. You know how my past relationship ended. It's hard to believe the best when I'm confronted with the worst."

"I'll prove it to you. There is nothing between me and Lauren." He glanced over my shoulder and stiffened.

I turned and stared into the icy glare of Lauren. Heath's reaction to her hearing his words looked guilty to me.

5

*H*eart heavy, I pasted a smile on my face, put a Halloween makeup of a bullet hole on my forehead, and stepped into the dining hall. All heads looked up from their tables in anticipation. In the spirit of the masquerade, Heath slipped into the room from the opposite door.

"Good evening! Welcome to our first murder mystery party. I'm your coordinator, Shelby Hart, and I will play the victim. Since I'm dead, I cannot answer any of your questions. Your job is to find out how I died, where I was killed, and who killed me. Think of the game Clue." I glanced around the room, hoping

Teresa's killer was there and that they wouldn't make the game I played a permanent one.

"Mingle, enjoy dinner and the atmosphere, and find justice for my death!"

The room rang with applause.

"It's quite easy to see how you were killed, darling." Grandma pointed at the bullet hole in my head.

I wiped at a smear of white powder at the corner of my mouth. "Is it?" I couldn't make things too easy for them. "I'm dead, remember? No talking to me."

Grandma huffed and stalked away, headed for the group of men she hung around with when Detective Ted was absent. I shook my head and decided to mingle silently so the participants could get a good look at me.

Across the room, Lauren, in a flapper dress of scarlet, caressed Heath's cheek. He drew back as if she'd burned him.

Good. Maybe he was telling the truth about their relationship.

"Hold up, girlie!" Bob, Marvin, Harold, and William swarmed me. "The Poker Boys need a good look. We aim to win this game."

"Poker boys?"

"We now hold a weekly poker game. If you're good, we'll invite you to play." Bob turned my face from side-to-side, then scribbled something on the paper in his hand.

William swiped my lip, then stuck his finger in his mouth. "Oh, you're a tricky one!"

Gross. I stuck my hand in my sparkly clutch, and reapplied the "powder" to the corner of my lip. With a smile, I gave a jaunty wave and continued around the room. So far, I'd heard nothing about Teresa.

Mom tapped me on the shoulder. "Shot in the kitchen by the chef because you criticized his cooking."

I cocked my head. "You have to write your guess on a slip of paper and wait until the end of the party." I leaned close to her ear. "Keep trying."

"But I really want to win that wooden box. You know I've admired it for months."

"Keep trying." I stepped away.

"Very funny." Heath waved his background papers in my face, and whispered, "Killed by a jilted lover? I've never been jealous in my life."

"Then act as if you were." I grinned.

He huffed. "You could give me some lessons." He stormed away.

There was a lot of talking for me being dead. Alice waved to me from the other side of the room. I squeezed through people questioning each other, pleased that everyone was having so much fun.

"No one is talking to our new

residents," she said.

"Well, I can't. I'm dead."

She looked at me as if I had turned green. "Fine. I'll lead them around the room and introduce them." She teetered on heels too high for the era we were supposed to dress in and hooked an arm through each of the new men's arms. Good. I couldn't eavesdrop as well if I were playing babysitter.

"The maid killed you in the sauna."

"Mom! Stop asking me. And, no, wrong again."

She groaned and left to join Grandma. If I'd known she liked the box so much, I would have given it to her a long time ago.

Once the buffet was filled, everyone took a break from the questions and piled their plates. I nibbled as I wandered the room, knowing most interesting conversations took place over food.

"What do you make about the killing

of our receptionist?" Bob asked the other Poker Boys.

"It has to be one of us," William said. "The girl hardly left the grounds. It was almost as if she had no life."

"That delivery boy was her beau," Marvin said, popping a deviled egg into his mouth. "Maybe he killed her."

The others looked at him with wide eyes. "How do you know that?" Bob asked.

Marvin shrugged. "I've seen the lad leaving her cottage in the early hours of the morning a time or two."

They all glanced to where Scott sat, alone, at a table for two.

"Nonsense," Harold said. "The boyfriend is too obvious."

I agreed, but in real life it was often the one closest to the victim who did the deed. When talk moved to their next poker game, I continued on.

"What do you do, Damon?" Alice sat

with the two newest members.

"I'm retired now. Made a fortune designing jewelry, then sold out."

"Yep," Alan added. "Made mine with youtube videos. It's time to sit back and enjoy life."

"There are some here who wonder what brings such affluent gentlemen to our humble surroundings." Alice glanced from one to the other.

"Why not?" Alan shrugged. "The cottages are comfortable, there's fishing in the creek, and easy access to town."

Alice beamed. "We do try to satisfy."

"You're doing a good job." Damon toasted her with a glass of red wine. "Do you do these type of activities often?"

"We try to have a social get-together every weekend. Shelby does a fine job, doesn't she?"

"The gardener? She's a really pretty gal," Alan said. "Is she single?"

"Very."

I wanted to throttle her! She knew darn well Heath and I were seeing each other, sort of. Of course, if I were in the market for an older man, which I wasn't, I could do worse than two handsome rich men.

I spotted Heath talking to Grandma. From the amused expression on his face, she was trying to determine whether he was the one who had killed me. I hoped she wouldn't win. People would think the game was fixed.

"I've got it." Lauren sauntered toward me. "You were poisoned by the handyman in the garden." She grinned.

"You have to write your guess on a piece of paper and put it in that box over there." Did no one read the instructions?

"Oh, I'm not playing for real. It's just so obvious."

I really disliked her. "I suppose since you aren't a permanent resident, you can't play anyway. Too bad." I gave her a simpering smile and strolled away.

It was time for me to disappear and stay at the spot where I was killed. I motioned to Alice to send the residents looking in ten minutes.

Kicking off my shoes, I raced for the patch of lush grass I'd chosen as my final place. No hard pavement or packed dirt for me.

I lay on my back, shoes next to me, and stared at the stars. Rather romantic if I hadn't been alone. Alone. In the dark. With a killer on the loose. I really hadn't thought this through.

A rustling in the bushes sent imaginary bugs tracking up my arms and legs. I was fine. The area would be swarming with people in a few minutes.

Footsteps alerted me to get into character. I kept my eyes wide and stared heavenward.

"Just the little lady I was looking for." Alan Barker peered down at me. "Since you're pretending to be dead, would you slap me if I stole a kiss? You lying there like Sleeping Beauty is more temptation than I can resist."

Seriously? Gag. "I wouldn't, if I were you."

"The dead damsel speaks and ruins the façade." He ran his hand up and down my arm.

"You do realize I'm not really dead, right?" I slapped his hand away.

"Of course, but fantasy is fun, don't you think?"

I rolled my eyes and chose to ignore him. I had my Tazor in my clutch. If he tried anything, he'd be twitching on the grass beside me.

"I found her!" Birdie knelt next to me and wrote on her paper. "I'm going to win!" She placed a hand on Alan's shoulder and pushed to her feet before racing back to the main building.

Fifteen minutes later, I rejoined

everyone in the dining room and removed the sticky bullet hole from my forehead. Opening the box, I said, "If you followed directions, wrote your deductions, and signed your name, then I will award the prize. In the case of a tie, I have a bonus question."

I scanned the answers. Three people had the answer correct. "Birdie, Damon, and...Leroy, (our resident vampire who only came out at night) have the correct answers. I was poisoned in the garden by the handyman. The gunshot was overkill. Now, for the tie breaker. Why was I killed?"

"You caught him in a murder," Damon said. "I'd kill for that, wouldn't you?"

"Not on your life," Leroy said. "She cheated on him, not that Shelby is that type of girl."

"She broke up with him," Birdie said, shooting to her feet. "Does no one watch what goes on around here? It's quite clear Heath is now keeping company with the interior decorator."

"All very good answers." I avoided looking at Heath. "The winner is...Birdie!" I handed her the box. "This was fun. Enjoy your dessert everyone."

Applause filled the room. I'd come up with a winning event for sure. Not that I'd garnered much information on Teresa's death, but hopefully, once I relaxed alone in my cottage, something would come to mind that had seemed insignificant when I first heard it. With my part finished, I left and headed home.

"Wait up." Birdie bustled toward me. "Did you learn anything about Teresa's murder?"

"What makes you think I was looking?"

She propped her fists on her skinny hips. "Seriously, Shelby. You must think I'm ignorant. Everyone knows that successfully solving a murder puts a bug under your skin. So, did you learn anything?"

"Not a thing. Good night." I hurried down the path. I had no intentions of telling anyone outside of family that I was investigating. The last time, things hadn't gone very well when I had.

"Psst." Someone hissed from the bushes.

I turned. "Don't scare me, Leroy."

"Here." He handed me a slip of paper and faded back into the shadows like the creature of the night he was.

I unfolded and read, "Men came and went from Teresa's cottage at all times of the night. One of them killed her." The least he could have done was told me who they were or given me a description.

I slipped the paper into my clutch and pulled out my key. As I inserted it into the lock, something hit me in the back of the head, dropping me to my knees. Another hit and I was out cold.

6

I came to with Heath, Alice, Office Ted, Mom and Grandma all peering down at me as if I were some weird specimen in a jar. "If people don't stop hitting me, I'm going to forget who I am." I struggled to a sitting position.

"What part of stay out of my investigation do you not understand?" Officer Ted held out a hand to help me to my feet.

"I was doing nothing more than unlocking my door." Which, surprisingly was unlocked and standing wide open.

"I opened the door, sweetie," Grandma said. "I was going to drag you inside, but decided—"

"To let the world know I was attacked." I put a hand to my head, bringing it away sticky with blood. "Ugh."

"Here." Heath swooped me in his arms and carried me to the sofa. "Should we call the paramedics."

"Already done." Mom propped a pillow behind me. "You're going to get blood on this, but it can't be helped."

Sirens wailed in the distance.

"You're bad for business, Shelby." Alice crossed her arms. "Nothing like murder or assault ever happened until you came along."

"You're welcome. Life must have been boring." I closed my eyes against the spinning room. Since the room remained silent, I peeled open one eye. Yep, they were all still staring at me. "What?"

"You're investigating."

"You need to stop."

"I ought to fire you."

The comments were fired at me with bullet precision. I sighed and decided to pretend I really was dead.

"How long has she been unconscious?" A new voice said.

"I'm not. I'm trying to pretend none of these people are here." I opened my eyes.

"Can you sit up?" The paramedic, a man too handsome to be dealing with blood, helped me sit. He took a look at my head. "I don't think you need stitches, but you'll need to see a doctor. I'm sure you have a concussion."

"I'm fine. I know the drill." Unfortunately, I'd been in this predicament before.

After bandaging my wound, the paramedics left. "The rest of you are free to go."

"Not me." Mom crossed her arms. "I'm staying here and waking you every thirty minutes to make sure you do wake up."

"I'm sure that's an old wife's tale."

"Nevertheless. Heath, take her to bed."

He chuckled. "Gladly." He picked me up again and carried me to my room where he laid me gently on the bed. "Your mother has a way with words."

"Doesn't she?" My face flamed.

"Can I get you anything?"

What I really wanted was a kiss. But, I reminded myself I was guarding my heart so shook my head instead. "I'll see you the morning, okay?"

I got the kiss anyway. He placed a tender one on my forehead and whispered, "Good night."

"I'll sleep right here," Mom said, patting the other side of the bed, "and set the alarm."

"I think I need to rest more than anything. Waking me up continuously defeats the purpose."

"This is what I did when you were a child. No need to stop now." She grabbed a nightgown from my dresser drawer and headed for the bathroom.

I took the opportunity to change into my nightclothes, swiped at my face with a makeup remover towelette, and crawled under the sheet. Staring at the ceiling, I contemplated who might have hit me.

The last person I'd spoken to was Leroy, and I couldn't see my friend knocking me out. He might be the strangest person at Shady Acres, but I'd bet my life he wasn't a murderer.

That left...I just couldn't see the Poker Boys killing anyone, but stranger things have happened in the realm of reality. Add those four with Scott, and the two newcomers, and I had seven suspects. Of course, her killer could have been a woman, but my gut told me the roses were from a man.

I must have fallen asleep because the next thing I knew, Mom was shaking me awake. "Okay."

The alarm went off at regular intervals all night until sometime right before dusk when Mom slept through it. I turned off the alarm, shoved it into a drawer and went back to sleep until ten a.m. when I was woken by a pounding on the front door.

"I'll get it," Mom mumbled, climbing from bed. "Glad to see you lived through the night. Sorry I fell asleep."

I groaned and climbed from bed, then shuffled to the kitchen as Mom opened the door and let Officer Ted in. "Questions?" Again, I knew the drill. Thank goodness I slept in shorts and a tee shirt.

"If you're feeling up to it."

"Sit. I'm making coffee."

"No, I'll do it." Mom shooed me to a chair opposite Ted. "Just as soon as I put on a robe."

She was back moments later, fully clothed, but hair in disarray and no makeup, and set to work making coffee. "Just a moment and it will be ready."

I shrugged at Ted. "What do you want to know?"

"Did something happen at your party to put a target on your back?"

"Not that I know of. I didn't participate, merely mingled so the people could get a good look at what killed me. I didn't ask any questions."

He wrote something on his notepad. "Did you see anyone lingering around your cottage?"

"Just Leroy. Oh, yeah. I'd forgotten." I reached for my purse that someone had left on the table for me and pulled out his note. I handed it over. "He gave me this. That's the last thing I remember."

"Looks like my next stop is Leroy's."

Grandma waltzed through my open front door. "Teddy!" She took his face in her hands and landed a juicy kiss on his lips.

"I'm in uniform."

"Oh, pooh." She waved aside his comment. "I've come to see what work my granddaughter has to do. I'll fill in for her."

"Work!" Mom dashed out the door, presumably to her job as receptionist.

Grandma shook her head. "She's going to have a heart attack when she realizes how she looks this morning."

"Rather than working the garden, maybe you could take her a hairbrush and some makeup," I offered. "I'm going to lie back down for a while."

"Come on, Ida." Officer Ted put his hand at the small of her back. "I'll walk with you as far as the main building. Take care of yourself, Shelby, and—"

"I know. Stay out of your investigation."

~

I didn't wake again until suppertime. Starving, I threw on a pair of denim capris under the wrinkled tee shirt I'd slept in and hurried to the dining hall. I shoved open the doors and skid to a halt as everyone turned to stare. You'd think I'd be used to being the center of attention, but I was far from it.

Flashing a grin, I grabbed a plate and piled it with a chicken breast, potato casserole, and asparagus. Trying to act as if getting hit on the head and sleeping away the day was perfectly normal behavior for me, I sat across the table from Heath and ignored everyone else.

"How are you feeling?" His eyes caressed my face.

"Much better. A bit of a headache, but that could be because I haven't eaten." I took a bite of my chicken. "You know what? I *am* going to investigate Teresa's death. I tried staying out of it, to no avail."

"I thought you'd already made that decision...against my wishes."

"Did I?" I shrugged. "I may have a bit of a memory lapse. Someone whacked me pretty good."

The expression on his face clearly said he didn't believe me. "I'll help you, but I won't like it. I have as much freedom around here as you do, so I can eavesdrop pretty easily."

"We need to find out who Teresa's admirer was." Relief that he was willingly helping filled me. Last time, he'd only helped because he had been the prime suspect, and that help had been given grudgingly. It seems the man doesn't like the thought of me being in danger. How sweet.

It wasn't my fault trouble followed

me like a dehydrated hyena at a watering hole. Not an appealing analogy.

"Teddy is very upset with you." Grandma set a giant salad on the table. "Nothing you say will convince him that you aren't being nosey again."

"I've decided to be nosey."

"Goody! My life is in the pits. I need something fun to do."

"We just had a party last night." How old was she? Sixteen?

"But, I didn't win. If we find this killer, we win. End of subject."

Heath's eyes widened. "Shelby is a chip off the old block. You're as crazy as she is, Ida."

"Hey, I resemble that." Grandma pointed her fork at him. "There's nothing wrong in seeking justice."

That depended on who you asked. "We need to be subtle. I don't want anything to happen to you."

"I'm a detective's girlfriend, or I will

be once he accepts the position. As detective, the boyfriend he already is. No one will dare bother me."

"I got reprimanded for being late." Mom joined us. "That Alice doesn't seem to think caring for my adult daughter was a good enough excuse."

I supposed she wouldn't. I turned to Heath. "How is Scott working out?"

"Better than Dave. The boy is a hard worker. It's almost as if he's trying to undo some wrong."

"Keep an eye on him. He's my top suspect."

"Scott wouldn't hurt a soul. I caught him releasing a rat from a trap this morning and letting it go in the maze."

"No! I'm going to start work in there." I shuddered.

"Not tonight," Mom said, narrowing her eyes. "Wait until morning. No wandering around after dark. Not anymore."

And Grandma was worried about Mom cramping her style. I was twenty-eight years old, not fifteen, and she still barked orders like a drill sergeant.

"Shelby, follow me, please." Alice stomped up and motioned her head.

"Looks like I've been summoned. Mom, would you box up what's left of my supper?"

When she nodded, I followed Alice to the small hall leading to the restrooms. "What's up?"

"First of all, how are you feeling?"

"Good, I—"

"Second, your mother needs to be at work on time or I'll have to fire her."

"I told her—"

"Third..." she shoved open the women's restroom. "Look at that!" She pointed to a message on the mirror written in red lipstick.

"Stay away, Shelbie." I pressed my lips together. No telling who the message was intended for. "They spelled my name wrong."

Alice crossed her arms. "I really have no idea what to do about you."

"Am I doing a sufficient job as gardener and event coordinator?"

"No complaints."

"Then, there's nothing you can do. This whole thing..." I waved my hand at the mirror, "has nothing to do with my job."

"But it has a lot to do with your life."

"I didn't know you cared." I smiled.

"We're friends, aren't we? Two women after the same man, brought together by a common bond? I don't think that message has anything to do with Teresa, and everything to do with Heath. I've seen Lauren wear that very shade of lipstick. What are we going to do about it?"

"Find a new decorator?"

"I can't. I signed a contract."

"Ignore her until she goes away?"

"I guess that's the best avenue." She sighed. "Clean that up." She marched away and left me to do the cleaning people's job.

I wiped off the lipstick and started to leave. Instead, I got a brilliant idea. I left a message of my own.

"Make me."

7

"*Go* do an inventory of the former receptionist's cottage." Lauren thrust a clipboard at me. "I don't care about personal items. Just those that belong to the community. What type of furniture, what does it look like, what condition is it in...you get the drill." She handed me a small camera. "Take pictures."

I started to protest, wanting to start work on the maze, but realized snooping through the victim's home might divulge clues the authorities had missed. "One hour. Remember our deal." I grinned as she scowled and fairly skipped from the dining hall in anticipation of a treasure hunt.

"Where are you headed?" Alice stopped me on the sidewalk.

"Lauren has sent me to inventory Teresa's cottage."

"Oh, good. She has no surviving family, so anything Shady Acres can use is to be set aside. The rest can go to charity."

"I'm only inventorying."

"Spend the day sorting. Whatever else you have planned to do can wait." She handed me a ring of keys on a stretchy wristband. "Keep these. I trust you."

I groaned inwardly. I'd never get the maze ready for a haunted treasure hunt at this rate. The way things were going, this weekend's soiree would be a simple pool party.

Hooking the ring of keys around my wrist, I set off, jingling, toward the worker cottages. The tape had been removed from Teresa's earthly home. I unlocked the door and stepped inside.

Wow. The girl might have been immaculate in her appearance, but her living conditions were horrible. Clothes lay scattered over every available surface. No dishes sat in the sink, but the garbage can overflowed with paper plates and plastic cups. This job would take more than a day.

I snapped a picture, then began laying all the clothes over the easy chair. I eyed some of the fashionable clothes, wondering whether Alice would let me buy them. Maybe the community could rally together for a yard sale to raise money for the restoration of the maze. I started a list of questions to ask Alice, then sorted through the Hollywood magazines on the coffee table.

I was going to need boxes. I texted Heath to find me some, then sent my questions to Alice. She responded quickly, saying a yard sale was a great idea and to make up a flier for the coming weekend. She also said I could set aside anything I wanted for myself and offer a fair price. Yay! My wardrobe needed updating and Teresa had been close to my size.

"Need help?" Heath appeared in the doorway, his arms loaded with boxes and packing tape.

"Do I!" I set him to work unfolding the boxes.

"This girl sure had a lot of...junk."

"It's not all junk. Her clothes cost a pretty penny." I put the stack of magazines in a box, clearing off the coffee table. Glass topped with a metal frame, it was in good condition. I snapped a picture of it and the blue and white sofa. One room down.

I then turned my attention to the clothes on the chair, choosing two dresses, a pair of jeans, and some capris in assorted colors for myself. The rest I folded and placed in a box.

Heath watched me for a while, then said, "What do you want me to do? I'm not very good at knowing what is valuable with women's things."

I'd actually forgotten he was there. "Here, take a picture of the dining set and anything in the kitchen that isn't dirty or in the trash. Then, wrap those knickknacks in paper and box them up." I would need to find someone to appraise them. They, too, looked expensive.

For someone wanting to save money, Teresa sure had spent a lot of it. Unless...I stepped back and looked at her things with new eyes. What if they were all gifts from admirers? Leroy had said men came and went from here. I needed to speak to him ASAP. But, since he slept all day and ventured out at night, I'd have to wait until after supper.

Once the front room was set to rights, and Heath was busy boxing up porcelain figurines, I moved to the master bedroom. Again, clothes lay strewn everywhere. I gathered them up and laid them across the bed, which, surprisingly, was made.

I chose a sparkly blue evening gown for myself, a pair of ankle boots from the closet, and some strappy silver sandals. Shopping spree done, I folded what was rest so Heath could pack them.

On the dresser was a large jewelry box. Another one hung on the back of the door. My eyes immediately went to a diamond choker. I snapped a photo with my phone and asked Alice if we could use it for a future prize.

She replied that the necklace would fetch a lot of money at a jewelers and to choose something less expensive. Fine. I chose a teardrop necklace with what I was sure was a fresh water pearl surrounded by smaller diamonds. I took another picture and sent it to Alice.

She said yes, but the rest would be sold. What a party pooper.

"How did someone with a receptionist job afford this jewelry?" Heath carried a few boxes into the room.

"My guess is they were gifts from a man. Maybe the very one who killed her."

"Should we turn them over to the police?"

"Why?" I stared at him. "They've already done their investigation in here. If they suspected anything, they would have taken it away."

He shrugged. "True." He set the clothes into a box, then started wrapping the jewelry boxes. "There's a lot of money here. We really need to find out who she was seeing. Not Scott. There's no way a delivery man could afford this stuff."

"Maybe he found out she was seeing someone else and killed her." I moved to the bathroom. Makeup and perfume bottles littered the counter. The makeup I tossed, any perfume at least half full could be sold. The yard sale would make a killing off Teresa's things alone.

I sat on the closed toilet lid and glanced at what was left of a vibrant young woman. Physical, material things that did her no good now.

What would I leave behind when it was my time for God to call me home? A few family members, if I went first, a couple of friends. I needed more. Sure, a few might remember I'd solved Maybelle's murder, and if I were as lucky, Teresa's, but was that enough of a legacy?

I wanted to get married and have children. I glanced through the door to where Heath packed. Did I want his children? They'd be pretty for sure, with wheat-colored hair and eyes as blue as the sky. Or maybe they'd have dark hair and hazel eyes like their mother. Either way, I wanted them.

Which meant I needed to not get killed finding Teresa's killer. I'd need to be discreet.

"Are you all right?" Heath knelt in front of me and peered into my face.

"Just thinking how sad it is that all that's left of Teresa is a few expensive clothes and jewelry." I blinked back tears. "No one should die a horrible death, much less die alone."

"You'll never be alone, Shelby." He squeezed my hands. "You have too many people who love you."

"Truly?"

"Truly." He planted a quick kiss on the tip of my nose. "It's almost lunch time. Let's finish up here."

"Thank you for your help. It would have taken me all day by myself."

He pulled me to my feet and smiled. "Any chance to spend time alone with you, even working, is worth the labor."

"Ha ha, it's like that is it?" I gave him a playful punch in the arm.

"Exactly like that." He tweaked my nose.

The lunch bell rang, reminding me I might have a response to my answer on the mirror. I plucked a tube of lipstick from the garbage, anxious to see Lauren's reply to my taunt.

8

*W*aving at Grandma as I passed through the dining hall, I headed to the women's restroom. Yep. In bright red lipstick were the words, "It's on."

I replied, "Bring it."

Excitement bubbled through me as I grabbed a plate from the buffet line. I filled it with fruit and a chicken salad sandwich.

"This little game you're playing in the restroom, isn't funny." Mom stepped beside me. "How do you know you aren't taunting a killer?"

"I don't." In fact, I rather hoped

Lauren was the murderer. How satisfying would it be to take her down?

"I've raised a...well, I don't know what I raised." Mom plopped into a seat at our usual table. "You keep me up at nights, Shelby."

"I'm sorry." I reached across the table and laid my hand across hers. "I don't mean to worry you, but these things just pop up."

She sighed and nodded. "I've decided to live here permanently. Alice has given me Teresa's cottage. Lord knows you need me here. So...I have a ton of stuff to sell in the yard sale. Do you think you and Heath could take some time today to help me box it all up?"

"What are you going to do with the house?" She was selling my childhood home?

"It's too big for me. I'm going to rent it for a while, then decide. Maybe you could buy it." Hope laced her words.

I could, probably. In fact, it was a great idea. "I will. Someday, maybe, I'll have a family and can move into it."

"That would make me very happy."

When Heath joined us, I explained how we needed his help.

"Of course. Alice will let us have the time since it's to raise money for Shady Acres. We can go right after lunch."

Since I planned on purchasing the house, and not sure that I wanted to rent it to strangers, I planned on leaving most of the furniture. Years of living within the four walls would provide a lot of things to sell without cleaning out the house.

~

I was exhausted from working on Teresa's cottage, but set to work with a vengeance anyway once we entered Mom's home.

She strolled through the rooms putting a red sticker on what she wanted moved to her cottage at the community, a blue for what stayed, and a yellow for what would go. Sadness clouded her features.

"I'll apply for a loan first thing Monday, Mom." I put an arm around her shoulders.

"Oh, sweetie. I'll just give it to you. I've enough money stashed away for the rent on the cottage. I don't know why I mentioned selling. It would break my heart."

"Would you mind if I rented it to Cheryl for now?"

"That's a wonderful idea. She'll take good care of our girl."

I smiled and placed a quick call to my friend.

"You bet I will! I'm sick of this apartment."

"Mom will be very happy."

"Glad we can both be thrilled. Now, fill me in on the latest at Shady Acres horror academy."

I laughed. "It isn't that bad. The place is really shaping up."

"I'm talking about the string of murders."

"I know." I told her about Scott, the two new residents, and the messages back and forth on the mirror.

"How deliciously evil. I want to play."

"I thought you couldn't get off work."

"I can't." She groaned. "But a girl can dream. I'll have to live vicariously through you."

"I'll call you anytime I have something new. Bye." I hung up and started boxing the things with yellow stickers. I missed investigating with my Amazon of a friend. Somehow, I felt safer with her by my side. At almost six feet tall, few people bothered her. Even in a burning building I hadn't been completely freaked out with her next to me.

We only took back what we were selling since Mom couldn't move in permanently until the cottage was renovated. For now, she was stuck with Grandma, and neither one was happy with the living arrangements.

We unloaded the boxes in the cottage that Mom would one day live in. I'd have to spend the next day pricing everything. At this rate, it would be too hot to play in the maze until autumn.

"What are you grumbling under your breath about?" Heath handed me a bottle of water.

"Too much work, too little time. I don't want to do this kind of work, I want to be in the garden or the greenhouse."

"I totally understand. I want to be repairing things, not carting boxes."

We sat on the sofa and finished our water, both lost in our own thoughts. "Maybe we should rebel," I said. "Tell Alice we aren't her personal servants."

"You never did finish reading all your paperwork, did you? It says 'and all other duties as assigned'. I don't think rebelling would accomplish anything but us losing our jobs."

No, I'd never finished the three inch stack of employee paperwork. Who had the time?

"This is a cozy picture." Lauren entered the cottage. "Sorry to break things up, but I need Heath."

I rolled my eyes.

"For what?" He said, tossing his empty bottle in a nearby trash bag. "This needs to be finished and ready for the yard sale this weekend."

"I need some things moved from Mr. Barker's cottage." The hard glint in her eyes said she wasn't taking no for an answer.

"Fine. I'll be back, Shelby." He brushed past Lauren and left.

She gave a coy smile. "I'll keep him busy for the rest of the day. Don't count on him coming back to help you any time soon."

I shrugged. "I'm sure I'll manage. Not every woman needs a man around constantly."

Her face darkened. She opened her mouth to say something, but turned and marched away instead.

I grinned. Score one for Shelby.

Remembering a few more shoe boxes on the top shelf of the closet, I headed to finish off inventorying Teresa's things before beginning the arduous task of pricing everything. I made my way around things that weren't here before. No doubt residents had been stashing their unwanted items here to be priced.

I ran my hand over a gorgeous oak roll top desk. Who would want to get rid of such a beauty? I opened the top to find it empty, then searched the drawers. Awesome! In one, I found a false bottom. Stashed inside were several envelopes.

I took them out and set them aside.

I'd need to go through them to make sure no one had thrown away anything important.

The boxes on the shelf in the closet held mostly tax papers and receipts. One had rose colored envelopes and stationary. I peered at the top sheet, noting indents of words. Locating a pencil, I rubbed it across the paper. Primitive, but effective.

"I'm sorry, darling. You know you're the only one for me. He's nothing but a boy compared to the man you are." I couldn't read fast enough. In my hand, I held proof that Teresa had a boyfriend. Perhaps the very person who had killed her. "I'll do anything to make it up to you. Meet me in our special place at nine o'clock."

I could only assume this was the time of her death. My hands shook. This needed to go to Officer Ted immediately.

The front door slammed. I shoved the

top sheet of stationary into my bra, pulled the closet door closed, and then hid behind the long dresses hanging there. I couldn't pinpoint why I felt the need to hide, only that my gut told me the person who had entered wasn't my friend.

Heavy footsteps passed through the house and into the bedroom, pausing in front of the closet.

I held my breath and scooted as far against the wall as I could. If they saw my feet, I was done for. Teresa hadn't worn a pair of rainboots in the entire time I'd known her, much less bright yellow ones with blue ducks on them.

The closet door opened.

I clamped my hand over my mouth to stifle a squeak.

The visitor rummaged through the few boxes left on the top shelf, then moved a few suit jackets as he, or she, picked through the pockets.

Please, don't see me.

Black loafers stopped in front of my hiding place, then turned and left.

I exhaled slowly. When I heard the front door open, I stepped out and peered into the bedroom. The stationary was gone from where I'd dropped it on the bed.

Whoever had been here had found what they wanted. What else had that person been searching for? The jewelry box was open, as were the dresser drawers. A quick glance showed that a pair of diamond earrings that matched the necklace I was using as a prize were gone. I'd meant to add them to the necklace.

"Shelby, you aren't going to get any work done standing around." Alice glared from the doorway.

"We've had a theft."

"What?" Her brow furrowed.

"Someone stole a pair of diamond

earrings not five minutes ago. Did you see anyone as you entered the cottage?"

She shook her head. "Weren't you in here?"

"I hid in the closet."

She tilted her head and gave me a patronizing look. "How can you stop a burglary if you're hiding?"

"I'm not ready to die today, Alice! My friends call out to me when they enter."

"Fine. I'll call Officer Ted. He's becoming a regular sight around here." She unhooked her cellphone from a clip at her waist and placed the call. "Yes, Shelby is at it again."

Seriously? Did these people actually think I did this on purpose? "At least it isn't another body," I mumbled.

"Now, she's talking to herself. I really think you need to get over here pronto." Alice pressed the hangup button and surveyed the room. "You are making very fast progress here."

"Can I borrow my mother to help price these things? That's going to be time consuming."

"Sure. We can forward calls to her cell phone."

"She doesn't have one."

"Then get her one, Shelby." Alice shook her head and left me to wait for Officer Ted.

He arrived within half an hour and stared at me from the front door. "You're giving me grey hair."

"You have a head of grey hair."

"Because of you."

"You had it the first time I met you." I crossed my arms and told him everything that had happened from the time I found the stationary.

He held out his hand and wiggled his fingers. "Good job."

Had he really complimented me? "I can't believe those words came from your mouth."

"I don't mind you stumbling across helpful information, I just don't want you going out to look for it."

I couldn't promise him, but I could promise I would tell him everything I "stumbled" across. "Glad we're working together now."

"We. Are. Not. Working together. Let me know if you hear anything about the earrings." He shook his head and left, taking the stationary with him. He stopped at the door. "Oh, I've assigned Heath the frustrating job of keeping an eye on you." He grinned and ducked out.

Frustrating? And why Heath? All that did was put him in harm's way. What I needed was an armed security detail.

9

Five a.m. and I was dragging things to the Shady Acres parking lot in anticipation of Booneville's largest yard sale. Already prospective buyers were lining up to view the items.

With the amount of people and items, we were sure to make enough money to repair the maze and have some left over. I put Mom in charge of taking payment so I could mingle and ask questions. I'd hoped for Heath's help, but Lauren had already snagged him for some trivial job she needed done.

He was supposed to take Teresa's

expensive jewelry to the buyer. Instead, the jewels hung around my neck in a pouch, making me feel extremely vulnerable. There had to be several thousand dollars around my neck.

By six a.m. no more cars would fit in the parking lot. Mom rang a bell and the stampede was on. Alice guarded the space between the sale and the lot like an English guard. We'd roped off what we could in hopes of keeping people from taking a five-fingered discount.

"Are you Shelby Hart?" A portly man with balding gray hair approached me. "I'm Luke Larson and I'm here to buy some jewelry."

"Jewelry?" Damon Markson and Alan Barker approached at a fast clip. "Is it real?"

"I have yet to determine."

"Yes, I'm Shelby." I untied the pouch from around my neck, glad to be free of its weight and led the buyer to a small table set off to the side.

Damon and Alan followed like children after candy.

I watched as Mr. Markson dumped the contents onto the table and rifled through the pieces. His face remained impassive, even as he held up an impressive ruby necklace.

Damon gasped.

Alan paled.

What was with these two?

"I'll give you ten thousand for the lot," Mr. Markson said.

That much? My knees buckled. "I'll take it."

"Wonderful." Alice clapped her hands. "That's a great start to our fitness gym."

"What gym?" I frowned, seeing more work that wasn't gardening in my future.

"The one I'm going to put in that vacant building. The one with the glass walls."

Oh, she meant the one hidden by overgrown juniper bushes. I sighed. No matter. The sale of the other items would help with hiring help to ready the maze.

Mr. Markson put everything back in the pouch, handed Alice a check, and then marched back to his vehicle. Damon and Alan followed. Soon the three were in a heated discussion.

I would have given my right pinky to know what they were talking about. Instead, I hurried to where Mom was waving frantically to get my attention.

"This woman is arguing about the price on this dress." Mom pointed at an elegantly dressed lady. "I told her those were real pearls on the neckline and the tag is still on the gown. It originally cost five hundred dollars."

"We won't take less than two hundred," I said. "I'm sure you'll agree that's a steal."

"Yard sales are supposed to be virtually free." The woman crossed her arms.

"I'm sorry, but we're trying to raise money for renovations. I'm sure I can find someone willing to pay the asking price."

"I will!" Another woman shouldered her way in.

Ms. Cheap shook her head. "Fine, I'll pay the two hundred."

"Two fifty!" the other lady said.

"Three hundred!" Ms. Cheap glared.

"Three fifty."

I pressed my lips together to keep from grinning. If they kept this up, we'd get the original ticket price. The dress ended up going to Ms. Cheap for four hundred. She took the gown and raced to the parking lot.

"Just as well," the other woman said grinning. "It wouldn't have fit me. I just like sticking it to rude people."

"And we thank you for that." I smiled and headed to where a young couple were rifling through less expensive clothes on another table. "May I help you?"

The young woman turned. "We just got married and are going on a cruise. I'm looking for a few nice things to wear."

"You look about the right size. Let me help you." Not that I'd ever been on a cruise, but I couldn't imagine any of the items not be suitable. Soon, the young couple had their arms loaded with sundresses, capri shorts and stylish tank tops.

"Stop that woman, Shelby!" Alice pointed to an elderly woman toddling toward a rusty car. "She stole a figurine."

I caught up to the woman. "Ma'am, did you forget to pay for the Hummel?"

"It's too expensive." She glowered. "My daughter collects these and doesn't have this one. Today is her birthday."

I glanced at the sticker price of thirty dollars. "Can you give me twenty?"

"Fifteen."

"Sold."

She slapped the money into my hand and hurried away. She'd gotten a rocking deal on something we should have sold for over a hundred dollars. Mom priced some things too cheap. A secret best kept from Alice.

By lunchtime, we were down to odds and ends. My feet ached, my back hurt, and my stomach rumbled. "Time to close up."

"I'll take everything that's left for one hundred dollars." A middle-aged woman held out a hundred dollar bill. "I'll even cart it away for you."

"Deal." I'd call the day a rousing success.

Alice took the money box from Mom and hurried for her office. "Come see me after lunch, Shelby."

I would. Right after I ate and checked my mirror message.

Heath and Lauren were already seated when I entered the dining hall. The witch sat in my seat! I grabbed a plate, filled it with food, and glaring at my usual table, went and sat next to Grandma with the Poker Boys.

"A rousing success of a sale," Bob said.

"Splendid." William raised his glass of tea to me in a toast. "Poker tonight? Five card draw. Five dollar ante. Come at seven and bring a snack to share."

"Sure." I shrugged. I didn't have anything else to do.

Grandma excused herself and left for the restroom. The Poker Boys pretty much ignored me after inviting me to the poker game. I glanced to where I normally sat.

Heath sent me an imploring look from

across the room.

I turned away. Man up and set the woman in her place, is what I wanted to say.

I finished my chicken salad sandwich and headed to the women's restroom. Today's message said, "Me one, you zero."

Twisting my lips, I tried to come up with something cutting to say. Zero was right. I had nothing.

"So, it is you leaving the messages." Grandma exited one of the stalls. "Who are you replying to?"

"Lauren, I think. It's a battle over Heath."

"No granddaughter of mine should fight over a man."

"She started it." I leaned against the sink. "I can't think of a reply."

"Say this." She handed me fuschia-colored lipstick. "When you use stink bait, you may get the biggest fish, but it will often be full of bones."

I choked on a laugh. "That will take me all day to write, but it's brilliant!"

"Sweetie, if you want to know how to put a woman in her place, all you have to do is ask. I'm an expert."

After writing Grandma's witty response, I knocked on Alice's office door and entered when commanded. She glanced up from her desk.

"Five thousand dollars, not counting the jewelry sale. You should open a resale shop."

"Gardening is fine with me." I sat in the chair opposite her. "What did you want to see me for?"

"I found this in the pocket of one of Teresa's coats. You must have missed it." She handed me a slip of paper.

"Fountain. Ten o'clock." More proof that Teresa had a boyfriend. Something we already knew. "I'll pass it on."

"Who do you think killed her?" Alice

leaned back in her chair.

"Right now...I have no idea. It has to be a man she was spending time with."

Alice shrugged. "I heard she spent time with a lot of men."

"Who told you that?" I really needed to find time to talk to Leroy.

"It wasn't a secret. I suffer from insomnia and wander the grounds late at night or early in the morning. I've seen men with my own eyes and heard things."

"What men?" I leaned forward.

"I respect our resident's privacy, Shelby."

"Even if one of them might be a killer?"

"I've given their names to Uncle Ted." She straightened. "The reason I wanted to speak with you was about the gym. Those bushes around the building need trimming. Heath is going to repurpose the wood floors inside. After that, we'll be ready to install equipment."

"But—"

"I know you're anxious to start work on the maze, but do this first. It shouldn't take more than one morning."

True, but what was the purpose of me making my own to-do list when Alice changed it up on me every single day? "Fine."

"You're attitude needs improving."

"Yep. Hire me a helper and I'll make a dramatic improvement." I left and headed for the soon-to-be gym.

The windows needed cleaning and a couple of hours with the hedger should take care of the hedge. A gym would be a nice addition and attract more clientele. Not that we had any empty cottages at the moment. Did Alice rent out the rooms in the main building? There were several vacant ones. All I'd ever seen stay there were temporary help. I could suggest she charge less rent and put the rooms to use. But that could wait until my attitude "improved".

I had a few hours before poker, so decided to pay Leroy a visit. I knew he slept during the day but it was early afternoon.

He answered the door, blinking against the harsh sunlight. "I expected you days ago."

"I've been busy. May I come in?"

He opened the door wider. "I made tea." He motioned to the small dinette table. "Let's talk." After pouring me tea into a cup, surprisingly feminine with pink roses along the edge, he sat across from me.

"Tell me more about Teresa's visitors." I sipped the orange pekoe tea. Leroy was a man of many surprises.

He peered at me over the rim of his cup. "I saw Bob a couple of times, Harvey, too. And...those two new guys were the most common visitors, other than that boy Scott."

"Really? Before they lived here? Was Teresa...charging for services rendered?"

"Where do you think she got all the nice clothes and jewelry? Not on a receptionist salary."

I wanted to ask if he'd pay her a visit, but held my tongue. "Did you ever hear her fighting with anyone?"

"I've heard raised voices a time or two, and Teresa crying sometimes when she was alone, but never could find out who she fought with."

"Hmm." Not a lot to go on. I could bring up the visits by Bob and Harvey during the poker game. I didn't think either of them were her killer, but they might have more information.

"Is this the same information you gave Officer Lawrence?"

"I told you a bit more." He grinned. "I'm not fond of police officers. I know they're necessary, but they aren't very understanding about my wandering around when most people are sleeping."

"I wouldn't imagine so." I chuckled and finished my tea. "Anything else?"

"Not at the moment, but I'll keep my eyes and ears open. Things have been pretty quiet since her death. This might be a tougher one to crack, Shelby."

"You're right. I don't know where to begin other than finding a discreet way of questioning Teresa's nightly visitors." A conversation that would make me very uncomfortable.

"You could always pose as our resident call girl." Leroy broke into laughter.

"Not funny." Even if I did have dreams of living a lavish lifestyle that isn't the way I would go about earning money. "Will you be at the poker game tonight?"

"Don't miss any. It's the only socialization I get." He escorted me to the door. "Be careful, Shelby girl. I count you as one of my few friends."

I smiled. "The feeling is mutual. I'll be as careful as I can be."

Which, considering I was about to accuse men of visiting a woman and paying her for her services, wasn't going to be very careful behavior.

10

*S*howered, with my pockets full of five dollar bills, and carrying a plate of sausage and cheese and crackers, I headed for Bob's cottage. Grandma met me halfway, carrying a tray of cheesecake bars.

"Glad you could make it," she said. "I'm usually the only female there."

"I doubt that bothers you much. What's Mom doing?"

"Watching a taped episode of one of her soap operas. Never could get into those myself. Real life is more drama than anything you'll find on television."

She opened Bob's door and waltzed in as if she owned the place. "The party has arrived!"

I laughed and set my contribution to the snacks on the kitchen counter before choosing my seat at the poker table. Counting me and Grandma, there would be six players. I hadn't played in a long time, not since Pink Poker nights with other teachers at Cooper Elementary, but I felt I could hold my own.

"How long do we play?" I set out my stack of fives.

"Until someone gets mad and quits," Bob said, grinning. "It's usually Harold."

"It is not." Harold glared. "It's William who quits first."

I sat back and listened to the men bicker. It ought to be an interesting evening. Especially when whiskey shots were passed around.

"No, thank you." I shook my head.

"My granddaughter is a teetotaler,"

Grandma said. "Barely tolerates a glass of wine now and then."

"Nothing wrong with that." Alcohol loosened tongues, which I was counting on, but that didn't mean I wanted to imbibe.

Bob dealt the cards, we anted up, and I glanced at two deuces, a king, a queen, and a three. Not a lot to work with. I turned over the queen and three. I was dealt a two and a king. I had this hand in the bag.

Doing my best to keep my expressive face neutral, I reached for my glass of ice water. When was a good time to ask these men about their visits to Teresa?

"Two pair." I turned over my cards and racked the thirty dollar pot toward me. Hello, new rain boots.

"First timer luck," Bob said, reshuffling.

I wiggled my eyebrows at him. "Let's do that again." From the look on his face,

I guessed it was Bob that had a tendency to quit first when things didn't go his way.

"Did Teresa ever join you guys?"

William laughed. "She played games of a different sort."

My smile faded. "Don't be crude. I've heard tales of you men joining in with her game. Don't be disrespectful of the dead."

"We're men, she provided a service." He shrugged. "But, she was a really nice gal."

Grandma's head whipped from one of her friends to another. "You all disgust me. Did you shower her with all those expensive gifts?"

"Us?" Bob looked taken aback. "We don't have that kind of money. Some of her other...friends, must have given her those."

I'd lost my enjoyment of the game. My heart ached for the poor girl who only wanted a better life. True, she went about it the wrong way, but she must have felt she had no other avenue.

"I've also heard one of her 'friends' abused her. Any idea who?"

Bob's face darkened. "If I'd have known that, I would have hunted him down. Teresa might have had loose morals, but she deserved to be treated well. She wanted to move to Hollywood and become a star."

I nodded. At least these four would have looked out for her had they known. How could I find out who she'd fought with?

"I know this is…private information, but it could be very important. Do you know who any of her other…visitors were?"

They glanced at each other.

"I've seen that new handyman, and the new residents, plus a few faces I don't know," Bob said, focusing on the cards in his hand. "I'm not proud of my behavior, Shelby, but my money helped her."

He could look at it however he wanted, it was still wrong. "Whatever helps you sleep at night." I threw down a royal flush and scooped up the pot again.

Bob groaned. "Let's break for snacks before she bankrupts us."

After our fill of finger foods and sugar, we sat back at the table. I lost the next two rounds, but since I was still ahead, it didn't bother me.

Grandma had been unnaturally quiet since the conversation about Teresa. I'd be sure to pick her brain on the walk home. It had to have come as a shock that her friends enjoyed a woman's company other than hers. Grandma had always prided herself on being the belle of the ball.

I leaned close. "Are you all right?"

"I've got a headache."

I suspected it was more of a heartache. "Sorry, gentlemen, but the ladies are leaving. Come on, Grandma. I'll walk you home."

The men glanced up, their faces creased with concern. It had to make Grandma feel better knowing they cared about her.

"Take care, Ida," Bob said. "I'll check on you in the morning."

She nodded, avoiding his gaze, and after dumping the snacks from my plate and hers onto another one of Bob's, rushed out the door.

Once the door closed behind us, I asked, "What's wrong?"

"I'm a silly old woman. Old being the main word here." Her heels beat a steady rhythm on the flagstone sidewalk. "I'm pouting because my friends chose a younger woman, not that I would offer what she did, but..."

I patted her arm. "I know."

"Men are scum. Most of them, anyway. Thank the Lord above for my Teddy."

I thought of Donald, the man who ditched me at the altar, then of Heath. Yes, fine, honest men were hard to find.

"I will make you sorry!" A shrill voice caused us to stop in our tracks.

I grabbed Grandma's arm and dragged her behind a thick bush near the pool.

"I'm really sorry," Heath said. "But I've tried to tell you nicely that we're over. You have some kind of mind block."

"Is it a crime to love you?" Tears poured down Lauren's face.

I wanted to gloat, I really did, but instead, I felt sorry for her.

"I care for someone else. No one forced you to cheat, Lauren."

"You prefer that Shelby over me?" Her voice rose.

"Yes. It's really not a hard decision for

me."

My heart leaped. He was finally putting her in her place.

She screamed and two-hand shoved him backward into the pool. With a nasty expletive, she slammed through the pool gate.

Without a second thought, I barged into the pool area and jumped into the pool. Throwing my arms around Heath's neck, I almost drowned us both.

"You heard, huh?" He grinned, shaking his head like a wet dog.

"The best words I've heard in a really long time." I rested my cheek against his chest. "You do know she'll make our lives miserable."

"Let her try." His arms tightened around me. "I'm sorry I wasn't tougher to begin with."

"Better late than never."

His chest rumbled with laughter.

I lifted my face. "Kiss me until I can't

breathe."

"I can't breathe just from having you close." He lowered his head and placed his lips on mine.

We'd had some wonderful kisses before, but nothing like the heated one that night in the pool. His kiss shoved all the fears and uncertainties aside, sending me soaring closer to heaven than I'd ever been. I didn't want the kiss to stop.

A pop sounded next to us. Water sprayed.

Heath fell backward. A dark stain spread around him.

Grandma rushed forward like an avenging angel and broke the glass plates over Lauren's head.

The woman dropped her pistol and crumbled to the ground.

"Heath!" I dove after him.

Slipping my arms around him, I struggled until I had dragged him to the pool steps. "Call 911."

"Already done." Grandma waded into the pool and helped me pull him out.

"I'm fine. She just grazed my arm." Heath grunted and lay on his back. "I don't think this was what you meant about her making our lives miserable."

"No." But, it did raise her higher on my list of suspects. If she could attempt murder to the man who had jilted her, maybe she had killed Teresa because the younger woman had stolen another man of Lauren's.

"Teddy is on his way." Grandma fell into a lounge chair. "Life is not boring at Shady Acres." She put a hand over her heart. "Maybe it's time for me to slow down."

Heath grinned. "Never, Ms. Ida. You're much too young." He pushed to a sitting position. "I would like to borrow your lovely scarf though."

"Very well." She sighed. "I'm tired of

it anyway." She unwound the silk rose-colored scarf from around her neck and handed it to him. "Tie it tight."

"Yes, ma'am." He winked at me.

We sat there, keeping a close eye on the unconscious Lauren until Teddy arrived.

When he did, he glanced at the prostrate woman and rushed to Heath's side. A moment later, a paramedic joined us.

"I knocked her out," Grandma said. "You should have seen it. But, now, I'm feeling rather faint." She toppled over.

Everyone forgot Heath and hurried to her side.

The paramedic took her pulse and radioed for a gurney. "I think she's having a heart attack."

Oh, that would kill her. Not the way one would expect, but because it was another sign of her advancing age. I gripped her hand. "Hold on, Grandma.

We're here."

"Stop fussing and take care of Heath. I'll be fine. It's just a spell."

"You're more important than a graze, Ms. Ida." Heath leaned over her. "It looks as if we'll share an ambulance."

I frowned.

"I'm playing along to make her feel better," he whispered.

"I can still hear you, and I appreciate the gesture." Grandma closed her eyes as the paramedic lifted her. "Where's Lauren? I hit her hard. She can't have wandered far."

Teddy groaned and took off like a horse at a starting gate.

Before I knew it, I found myself alone next to a blood stained pool deck with a crazed woman on the loose. To top it all off...she'd taken her gun.

11

*F*ully expecting a bullet in the back, I raced to Mom's cottage and pounded on the door. "Hurry! Let me in."

"For Pete's sake." Mom, dressed in a robe over a cotton nightgown, opened the door.

"Grandma had a heart attack, Heath's been shot, and there's a crazy woman with a gun running loose." I collapsed onto the sofa. "Get dressed and drive me to the hospital, please."

"You're bleeding." She pointed at my arm.

With the rush of adrenaline, I hadn't

noticed the bullet had grazed my upper arm before striking Heath. I sure noticed it now. Pain burned through me. My stomach churned. "I guess I need something to wrap around the wound."

It wasn't surprising that I'd been forgotten in all the hullabaloo.

Mom tied a dish towel around my arm. "Sit tight. I'll be right back. Don't die on me."

I laughed, which hurt. I didn't plan on dying, and doubted a scrape I hadn't noticed at first would finish me off. "I'll be here."

She returned within five minutes and another three had us speeding toward the hospital. She pulled up right in front of the Emergency Room doors. "We need help here!"

Waving off the approaching medics, I walked into the building on my own two feet. "I'm here to see Ida Grayson and Heath McLeroy."

The nurse eyed the bandage around my arm. "They're in a room together. I'll add you to the party. Follow me."

She led me to a room where another nurse stitched Heath's arm and Grandma lay on a bed. The atmosphere was filled with laughter, immediately dissolving my worry.

"Wait." Heath narrowed his eyes, pushing the nurse's hands away. "Shelby, you're injured."

"Same bullet that got you, I guess." I plopped in the last available seat. "How are you two feeling?"

"Peachy." Grandma winked at the young resident who entered the curtained off cubicle. "There's quite a bit of eye candy around here."

"Now, you behave, Mrs. Grayson." He checked her stats.

"This is my granddaughter, Shelby. She would make a good doctor's wife."

"Hey." Heath glowered. "Don't go

marrying her off. I'm sure I've a bit of her blood in me now. That makes us practically one person."

The resident glanced at me. "We'll take care of you next, Miss."

"I'm in no hurry." Except for the pain. I couldn't believe how much my arm burned. "Some Tylenol would be nice."

Officer Ted joined us. "She got away. I'll need you three to be very careful until we catch her. She won't take kindly to Ida breaking a plate over her head."

Or me stealing Heath. I grinned, remembering again the words he'd said to get rid of her.

"Your turn." The nurse peeled off the dishtowel and handed it to Mom. "Want this?"

"Nope." She took it between two fingers and dropped it in the trash. "Why does all the excitement happen when I'm in bed?"

"Because you go to sleep with the

sun," Grandma said. "How are you going to find another man living like that?"

"I don't want another husband."

"I'll take care of it."

I shook my head and met Heath's amused glance.

The nurse cleaned and dressed my superficial wound. "Keep it clean. You'll have a light scar to show off."

My very own battle wound. Two hours later, release papers in hand, we piled into Mom's car, and headed home. Officer Ted followed in his squad car to take our reports. I really needed to just make copies of one report and hand him one every time he came around.

We congregated at my place, which seemed to be the norm. Mom made tea, of course, and the rest of us sat anywhere there was room.

Before he could ask, I told Officer Ted what had transpired, with Grandma and Heath injecting their own versions.

"Shelby Hart, you need your own police department to keep up with you."

"Think of it as job security," I said, smiling. "And of how much I enrich your life."

He laughed, actually laughed. It might have been the first time I'd witnessed such a thing from him. "That you do."

"I'm sorry you were hurt." Heath snuggled me close under his good arm. "I should have noticed."

"Why? I didn't until Mom said something." I stared into his eyes. "I'm glad things weren't worse. Where do you think Lauren went?"

"I told Ted about a cabin she goes to in the mountains. Maybe he'll find her there and we won't have to worry anymore."

"Do you think she killed Teresa?" That would make things easy and finished.

"I don't see a motive."

Neither did I. Still, I wouldn't discount

her as the killer. It also didn't look as if the cottages would be renovated any time soon. Lord, I hoped Alice didn't give me that particular job.

I closed my eyes and fell asleep on his shoulder.

When I woke, I was alone, on the sofa, covered with a light blanket. I sat up and tested the use of my arm. Sore, and a bit of pulling, but nothing too bad.

I readied myself to start the day then headed to breakfast, mentally going over my to-do list. First thing, I wanted to clean the bathroom mirror. There would be no more messages. Second, I needed to hire someone to clean the maze and start trimming.

With the money the yard sale had brought in, there was no reason to do the work myself. I had other things to occupy my time.

I waved at my family and headed for the bathroom. My blood chilled. Written on the mirror were the words, "It isn't over yet."

Seriously? How did Lauren do this and not get caught? I snapped a photo with my cell phone. Should I reply or let the dangerous game die? I decided to let it die and wiped the message away.

Back at the table, I showed Heath and the others the picture of the message. "Do you think she did this before taking off?"

"Or she's hiding close by," Heath said. "We have to let Ted know."

I nodded and sent him a copy of the message via text, and explained about the ongoing game. His reply, "Stop doing things like this! Do you have a death wish?"

I smiled and slipped my phone in my pocket as Mom set an omelet in front of me.

"Let me serve you, my injured chick."

"Thanks. You're the best Mom ever."

"I know." She patted my shoulder and sat down.

As I glanced around the table, I realized I was the luckiest girl in the world. Then, I lifted my head to see Alice motioning me over. With a sigh, I pushed to my feet and went to see how she would disrupt my day.

"What happened to you?"

I explained about last night, leaving out Heath's declaration of love. Why rub salt in the wound?

"Why am I just now finding out about this? I'm the manager!"

"I'm sure you were asleep. Why wake you?"

"You frustrate me. Anyway, I need you in my office. I have a list of things to work on."

Of course. "I'll be in as soon as I finish my breakfast."

"Very well." She turned and headed for the elevator. "Bring Heath with you," she tossed over her shoulder.

Half an hour later, Heath and I sat across from Alice's desk. She handed us both packets.

"There are still several areas of this community that need attention. I assume Shelby will be working on the maze now that it's clear. Heath, I need you to repair the boathouse. I'd like to purchase a couple of fishing boats and kayaks."

"We have a lake?" My head jerked.

"Have you still not read your employee papers, Shelby?" Alice spit the words. "Yes, we have a lake. We will soon have an exercise room and a functioning maze. Why must I do everything myself?"

I shrugged. "If you didn't keep me so busy from sunup to sundown, I might have time to read those papers."

"Make it a priority. Failure to do so can result in dismissal of your duties."

I seriously doubted she'd fire me.

Where else could she find someone who does all that I do with little complaint? Notice I didn't say no complaint. Somedays, I was the queen of complaint.

"With your permission, I'll be hiring workers for the maze. That job is too big for me."

"Fine. Heath, once you have a chance to look at the boathouse, let me know what you need."

"I've seen it. It needs a complete overhaul. I figure Scott and I can rebuild it within a week."

"That's how I like my employees to act." She cut a sharp glance at me.

"I can have the maze done in a week...with help. I'll hire some today." Gosh. I wasn't a miracle worker.

She released us shortly, armed with a packet containing enough jobs to last through the summer. I counted it job security.

"Want to visit the boathouse with

me?" Heath slung his arm around my shoulders.

"Sure. I can hire some workers as we walk." Three ought to do it. I called a temporary agency I trusted, got the promise of three men starting tomorrow, one with a backhoe, and continued happily alongside my guy to the boathouse.

"You weren't kidding about a new build." The shack listed to one side and contained holes large enough to put my head through.

"We'll have to tear it down and start fresh, but the two boats inside are serviceable." He opened the door.

I cringed as it creaked on rusty hinges. Inside, my gaze immediately fell on a sleeping bag and coleman stove. "We have to leave now." I tugged on his arm. "We need to get Officer Ted. This is where Lauren is staying." I had no intention of seeing her gun again.

"Are you sure? In a shack?"

"She's deranged."

We hurried away, my fingers already dialing Officer Ted. I don't know why I couldn't bring myself to simply call him Ted like everyone else. It had to be the uniform.

"I'm on my way. Don't touch anything."

"We've already left the building."

Heath led me to a bench close to the cottages. "We should be relatively safe here."

"She did shoot us at the pool last night. We aren't safe anywhere."

"Good morning!" Alan Barker, a backpack slung over one arm and his other hand clutching a thick stick, strolled toward us. "I just learned we have a hiking trail that skirts a lake. Ciao!"

"Should we stop him?" I craned my neck as he disappeared into the trees.

"Lauren's beef isn't with him. The best thing we can do is avoid her at all costs."

No argument from me. "There's the calvary." I stood to welcome Officer Ted.

"Show me," he said.

We made our way back to the boathouse and stood around while he went inside. I'd never felt more vulnerable. A bullet could come from the trees at any moment. One that would finish off me or Heath.

I stepped in front of him.

He shoved me behind him.

I giggled and stepped in front again.

"If the two of you are finished doing some weird tango, I'm ready to head back," Officer Ted said.

"Is it her?" I asked.

"Only forensics can say for sure." He ushered us ahead of him. "Until then, maybe you should stay away."

"I have to rebuild," Heath said.

"Then don't come here alone. Ever."

He nodded. "I can promise that."

"Shelby doesn't count."

I made a noise in my throat. The only reason I would hang around the boathouse in the first place was to spend time with Heath. But, since my own list was as long as the Arkansas River, I'd stay busy.

I glanced back once more and spotted Alan watching us from the tree line. He gave a salute and ducked into the shack.

12

With workers repairing the maze, and Heath busy supervising the boathouse reconstruction, I was free to take my first day off in weeks. I was supposed to have Sundays and Mondays off, but somehow that never seemed to happen.

I led Mom and Grandma to my Volkswagon. Grandma stopped.

"I'm not riding in a bug. Besides, it's too small. Where will we put all of our packages?"

I rolled my eyes and switched direction toward Mom's dilapidated van. "You need a new vehicle, Mom."

"Not on my salary."

Maybe not, but on what Cheryl was paying for rent, she could. I climbed into the backseat, and clicked my seatbelt into place.

After all the clothes I had picked from Teresa's things, I didn't really need a trip to the mall, but wouldn't pass up an opportunity to spend time with the two most special people in my life without someone trying to kill me. Maybe, I'd find a new pair of rain boots and/or floppy hat. That was enough to spur excitement for me.

An hour later, Mom parked in front of the mall and we piled out, giddy on the high of shopping. "We need to do this more often."

"Maybe not shopping," I said, thinking of my bank account, "but definitely girl time away from Shady Acres."

"Don't bash our home, girl." Grandma

tapped me on the shoulder. "I love it there. Especially now with all the new amenities. The best thing the new owner did was hire Alice as manager. She might be like salt in an open wound, but she gets the job done."

"She's a great delegator." I hitched my purse onto my shoulder. "So, shall we start at one end and wander?"

"Yes," they said in unison.

It was going to be a long, wonderful day.

Grandma exited the dressing room of the first upscale boutique. "Well?" She twirled.

Mom and I glanced at each other. How could I kindly tell her that the strapless gown was more suited to a twelve year old who had yet to have need of a bra rather than a close to seventy-year-old who had an ample bosom? Not to mention the dress was mustard yellow and did nothing for her complexion.

"I can see from your expressions that it's not for me." Grandma sent us a dirty look and ducked back behind the curtain.

"She really needs to act her age," Mom said.

"I heard that! Just because I don't dress like I have one foot in the grave doesn't mean I'm not a mature woman."

Mom hadn't actually said that at all. "Try on the next dress, Grandma. Maybe it will be better suited for...your skin tone."

"Oh, was that all? They have the same dress in cherry red."

"Now, you've done it." Mom sighed, and lowered her voice. "Can you imagine being her daughter?"

"I would have laughed my way through high school."

Grandma didn't bother trying on the red dress. Instead, head held high, she marched to the counter and purchased it. Once she had, she thrust the bag at me. "Early Happy Birthday." She grinned.

"Really?" The dress would fit my slimmer figure very well. "When would I ever wear it?"

"I think the proper response is thank you."

"Oh, I thank you very much." I draped the garment bag over my arm. Wait until Heath saw me wearing the lovely gown. His eyes would pop out.

"I'm hungry." Grandma led the way to the food court where the three of us split up to purchase the lunch of our choice before meeting at a table to the side of the court.

I set my salad down while Grandma set down a cheeseburger and fries. Mom ordered a chicken wrap.

"That is bad for your cholesterol," she said, motioning to Grandma's burger.

"Mind your own business."

"I have to look out for you."

"See how she cramps my style?" Grandma glanced at me with wide eyes.

I laughed and dug into my fully loaded taco salad. "I needed today, thank you."

"You're welcome. Now," Grandma rubbed her hands together, "let's talk about the case."

Mom and I groaned.

"There isn't a lot to tell." I glanced at the healing graze on my arm. "Nothing has happened in almost a week. Although, I did see Alan Barker duck into the shed the day we found the sleeping bag."

"Lauren's sleeping bag," Grandma said, pointing a French fry at me.

"Allegedly. But, since she has yet to show her face again, and she wasn't at the cabin Heath mentioned to Ted, we think she may have fled."

"Of course she fled. You don't shoot two people and stick around."

"The two of you scare my blood cold." Mom shook her head. "Want to know what I think?"

"Yes." I tilted my head. She rarely ventured her opinion on anything as dangerous as murder.

"I think she's close by and waiting to finish what she started."

"Kill me or Heath?"

"Yes." She avoided my gaze. "But...I do not think she killed Teresa."

"Why?"

"Her shooting you and Heath was spur of the moment. Whoever killed Teresa lured her to the maze. Thus, it was premeditated."

"Good observation." I needed to ask her opinion more often. "Where could Lauren hide close by?"

"There is fifty acres of wooded land surrounding Shady Acres. Not to mention the basement no one visits. I'm sure there are other hidey holes. This was quite the resort during Prohibition. You know how those people liked to hide the liquor."

"How do you know this?"

She glanced up. "It was in the new employee paperwork. Didn't you read yours?"

I groaned and shoved another bite of salad into my mouth. I barely had time to dive into the newest mystery novel much less a stack of boring papers. Although, I needed to, if they were also full of this type of information. "I'll finish reading them tonight."

"Look. There's that new resident Damon. He's dreamy," Grandma said.

"Twenty years too young for you," Mom said.

"Age is nothing more than a number. But, I've got my man. My eyes still work though. I figure I'll recognize a fine looking man until the Good Lord takes me home or takes away my sight."

"He appears to be very interested in us," Mom pointed out.

I'd noticed the same thing through Grandma's short speech. With the three of us staring back, he turned and strolled away. Now, why hadn't he come over and said hello? "Let's follow him." I tossed everyone's unfinished lunches onto a tray and slid them into the garbage.

"I wasn't exactly finished eating," Grandma said, "but okay. I'm always up for surveillance."

"There's very little you aren't up for," Mom replied.

"Hush, you two." I made a shushing motion with my hand. "He went into Hot Topic." Why would a single man go into a store for young women?

"Oh, I love that store." Grandma took a step forward.

I grabbed her arm and pulled her back. "Don't let him see you." I glanced around us, my gaze falling on a couple of teenage girls. "I'll give you ten dollars each to nonchalantly find out what that man is buying."

"Non...what?"

"Secretly."

"Done." They held out their hands.

"I'll pay after you bring me the information."

They darted into the store and peered around clothes racks. This wasn't illegal, was it? I'd hate to be arrested for influencing a minor.

We hid in an alcove near the bathrooms when Damon exited the store. Right behind were the girls, hands out.

"He bought two pairs of jeans and two tee shirts," one of them said. "Now, pay up."

I handed over the money and thanked them. "Women's clothes?"

She shrugged. "Couldn't see that. Do

they sell men's clothes in there?"

I had no idea. "Grandma?"

"Of course, they do."

Interesting. Now to find out whether the clothes he'd purchased were for male or female. I ducked into the store, bought a couple of things, then dashed back out. "Where is he?"

Grandma pointed. "Victoria Secret. I need to go in there."

"Wait a minute. I have an idea." I positioned myself right outside the door. When Damon exited, I turned and ran into him, knocking the bag from his hand. With a quick switch, I now held his Hot Topic bag and he had mine.

"Sorry. Oh, it's you. Hello."

"Shelby." His smile didn't reach the eyes that roamed over my body. "Enjoying your day?"

"Very much so. Bye." Motioning to the others, we entered the store.

While they shopped, I glanced in his

bag. Women's clothes. I raced after him. "Wait up."

He turned.

"My apologies, but our bags seem to have gotten mixed up." I held out his purchases. When we both held the correct bags, I rejoined Mom and Grandma.

"The clothes are for a woman."

"It isn't surprising that a man who looks like he does would be buying for a woman." Grandma held up a red lacy bra. "The straps can come off of this. It would go with that gown perfectly."

"You are not going to buy me underwear. I am not a child." Although, she was right. It would be perfect.

Wait a minute. "What are you cooking up? Why these sexy things that no one but myself will see?"

"A woman is sexy if she feels sexy. Lingerie makes you feel sexy." She winked at Mom, who crossed her arms and looked away, mumbling something about loose morals.

With more than one mystery to now occupy my mind, we made our purchases and headed to the next store where I found a pair of rain boots colored like a ladybug. Gorgeous!

"I have no idea why you wear those things. They aren't feminine in the least." Grandma held one out by her fingertips.

"I'm a gardener. This is what we wear."

"Whatever." She dropped the boot in the bag. "Let's head home before your mother drops dead."

Which, was Grandma's way of saying she was tired. So...we headed back to Shady Acres.

Once I'd put away my purchases, and the gifts from Grandma, I sat at my dinette table and started reading the papers I should have read weeks ago. Mom was right. Not only did they state employee rules, but the history of Shady Acres. Lauren could be hiding in any number of prohibition tunnels.

13

My phone rang right before supper on Saturday. "Hello, Grandma."

"No time for pleasantries. Wear the red gown to dinner and try to look hot, darling." Click.

I stared at the phone for a second. Why dress up? I didn't have anything special planned, despite the fact it was my twenty-ninth birthday. When I'd approached Alice about a community event, she'd shut me down saying we couldn't play favorites among the employees.

Now, I was either going to have to be

late for supper or endure Grandma's wrath. I chose to be late.

Half an hour later, dressed to the nines, as Grandma would say, I pushed open the door to the dining hall.

"Happy Birthday!" The residents, all dressed in formal wear, rose to their feet.

Tears sprang to my eyes, blurring the candlelight and sparkling stars hanging from the ceiling. I recognized the same decorations from our mystery dinner, but didn't care. My family and friends had gone to a lot of trouble for me.

"Happy Birthday." Heath placed a kiss on my cheek. "You look gorgeous." He crooked his arm.

"Thank you." I slipped my arm in his and let him lead me to our table.

"How was this accomplished without my finding out?" I asked as Heath pulled out my chair.

"Your grandmother threatened

everyone with bodily harm if they spilled the secret." Another quick kiss and he went to the buffet.

"I told the cooks that you love seafood, so it's a seafood extravaganza," Grandma said.

"Thank you. This is wonderful."

"Blink back the tears, dear, or you will ruin your makeup." She fanned my face with a napkin. "There will be dancing and testimonies after dinner."

No amount of fanning would stop my tears.

Heath brought me a plate piled with shrimp, a lobster tail, crab legs, and butter. "Here's a heart attack on a plate."

"Yum." I tucked a napkin into my bodice in what I knew was a vain attempt to keep butter from my dress, and popped a shrimp into my mouth.

Heath sat next to me. "Ida told me about Damon buying clothes at the mall. It turns out he has a daughter."

Darn. There went that theory. "I'll have to keep investigating."

"Not tonight, though. Tonight, the focus is all on you."

Which was weird. While I had selfish tendencies, I was human, after all, I usually kept attention off me and on someone else. I'd do my best to enjoy the celebration and return to being regular Shelby tomorrow.

After everyone had eaten, Grandma stood and tapped her spoon against her wine glass. "Now, we tell our Shelby girl how we feel about her. Keep it clean, she's a fuddy duddy." She sat back down.

"Really?" I scrunched my mouth.

"Don't do that. It makes lip wrinkles." Grandma took a microphone from a nearby stand. "Who is first? Alice?"

"As manager, I find that fitting." Alice took the microphone. "While Shelby is supposed to be our gardener and not a crime solver, I think we can all sleep better knowing that she is on the lookout for Teresa's killer." Alice handed the mic to Bob.

I cringed. Why didn't she just make the target on my back bigger?

"I suspect Shelby cheats at poker, but she's a bang up gal and a lot of fun. Happy Birthday."

I had just taken a drink of tea, which I proceeded to spew across the table.

"She does not cheat at poker," Harvey said. "And she brings good snacks. Catch Teresa's killer, girl, so we can get on with our lives. But, keep our secrets while you're at it."

And on and on it went. Residents extoled my virtues, spoke of my crime solving skills, a few flirted, some cracked jokes, until my head spun. Then, the microphone was handed to me.

I cleared my throat and stood. "I'm not a detective. I'm not even good at solving mysteries. Luck is my friend, as are all you. Tonight has been the best night of my life and I have every one of you to thank." I sat back down to applause.

"Let's walk." Heath took my hand and led me outside.

I glanced behind us. "Why is Ted following us?"

"Well…" Heath turned me to face him. "Lauren's DNA was all over the shack. Since I refuse to stay in my cottage, he has decided to be our bodyguard."

I glanced back again. "He really fears for your safety?"

"It appears so." He resumed walking.

"I finally read the employee paperwork. Did you know about the tunnels running under Shady Acres?"

"Yes. Ted has already checked them out. No sign of Lauren or that she's been there."

"Focusing on Lauren distracts from

finding Teresa's killer."

"You don't think they're one and the same?"

I explained Mom's reasoning. "It makes sense to me. We've nothing else to go on." This killer was patient enough to sit back and relax. The first time, Shady Acres employees had dropped like flies as if suffering from food poisoning served up at a picnic.

Maybe I was off in left field on this one. Maybe Teresa's death was a spur of the moment. It was likely Lauren came upon her after someone had given her roses, and then killed her. But...my gut told me Lauren wasn't Teresa's killer.

But then, why hide? Trying to shoot Heath had been a moment of rage...a crime of passion. I doubt he would have even pressed charges since our injuries were minor. My mind spun like the clouds over head.

"Uh, are we under a weather

advisory?"

Ted joined us as we stared at the clouds. "I just got an alert. We're under a tornado watch."

"Swirling clouds mean more than a watch," Heath said. "Where's the nearest door to the tunnels?"

"The only one I know of is behind the greenhouse."

How had I missed that? The air turned heavy and still.

"Take Shelby. I'll get the others." Heath raced back to the dining room at the same time we sprinted for the greenhouse.

The wind picked up as we struggled with a door I hadn't known was there. From the looks of the butchered bush next to it, it had been well hidden.

Pulling together, Ted and I managed to pull the door open.

"Shelby!" Lauren yelled from inside.

A gun rang out as Ted stepped in

front of me. He spun and fell.

I knelt next to him and felt for a pulse.

"I'm not hurt. Just bruised." He sat up. "Bullet proof vest."

"What do we do? Lauren will shoot people as they attempt to go down."

"I have to go after her." He glanced at the clouds. "Wait as long as possible, then send people down. They have a better chance with a bullet than a twister."

Maybe the twister wouldn't touch down. "You took a bullet for me. You do care."

"You're like the daughter I never wished I had." He grinned. "Don't tell Ida." He rushed down the stairs and into the darkness.

He could crack jokes all he wanted to, I now knew how much he cared. I stood behind the door and held it open, using it as a shield. More than likely, Lauren had run down the tunnels and away from us, but I wasn't taking any chances.

The wind increased. I glanced up as a funnel stretched from the cloud to the ground in the direction of the lake.

I waved my arms at Heath and the others. "Hurry!" The wind whipped the words from my lips.

The twister spun closer, threatening to toss my friends like confetti. I practically shoved Grandma and Ida down the stairs.

"Come on, Shelby." Mom peered up with wide eyes.

"I have to help."

"Leave her be, Sue Ellen," Grandma said. "Let Shelby be Shelby and you turn on your phone to provide some light."

The others rushed toward me. One elderly lady who stayed to herself most of the time fell. Birdie stopped to help her and slipped down next to her. Heath put an arm around each of their waists and struggled for the tunnel.

"It's coming!" It was all I could do to hold the door open. The wind pushed the rough wood against my back. I dug my heels into the dirt and held on.

Heath almost lifted the two women off their feet and stumbled down the stairs with them before coming back and closing the door. "Sit on the ground everyone."

I slid down the dirt wall, unmindful of my dress. I'd almost been killed twice and it wasn't even bedtime. First by Lauren, then by Mother Nature.

That really helped put things into perspective for a girl. As the wind howled above us, I glanced at the blue-tinged faces of those I loved as Mom and Grandma huddled around Mom's cell phone.

Heath sat next to me and pulled me close. "Are you all right?"

I nodded and explained what happened before he arrived. "I'm worried about Ted."

"I should go look for him."

"Not alone." I clutched his arm wishing I had my Tazer. "How would we get away without alerting Grandma?"

As if in answer to my question, Mom's cellphone blinked off. "Well, pooh. The battery is dead."

"The storm won't last long," I said. "I'll have Grandma help get the others back to their cottages, then we'll look for Ted." As long as we didn't hear a gunshot—could we over the noise of the storm?—he'd be all right, right?

As tornadoes usually do, the storm passed quickly. I got to my feet and waited while Heath opened the tunnel door.

"Grandma, please help these people home. I'm going to get a flashlight and search these tunnels."

She gripped my shoulders. "Bring back my Teddy, sweetheart."

"You knew?"

"Where else would he be? If he isn't with us, then he's chasing a crazy person down here." She thrust her purse into my hands. "Use my gun. Stay safe." She patted my cheek and ushered the others out like a mother hen.

Heath stepped back to my side. "Are you sure you want to do this? Ted is trained, we aren't."

"He took a bullet for me. He was wearing a vest, but he still stepped in front."

Heath took my face in his hands and kissed me. Long. Hard. Like a man starving. "That's in case it's the last time. When we get out of here, I'll kiss you breathless so you remember what it's like to live. Now, go get that flashlight."

I scampered up the stairs. Pausing at the top, I surveyed the downed trees and uprooted bushes. Just when the grounds were almost complete, the twister had given me a lot more work to do.

One of the backhoes from the maze sat smack dab in the middle of the vegetable garden. I sighed and unlocked the shed.

I grabbed a flashlight from a nearby shelf and hurried back to Heath. At first, my flashlight beam didn't spot him and my heart lodged in my throat. Then, he appeared from the shadows, and all was once again right with my world.

"Let's catch a crazy woman." He smiled and held out his hand. "Happy Birthday, Shelby."

"There's no one I'd rather chase a nut with." I took his hand.

14

*H*eath kept me tucked behind him as we neared a T-junction. He peered both ways. "I don't see anyone," he whispered. "Which way do we go?"

I shined the flashlight on the ground. "This way." I pointed right where two sets of what seemed to be fresh prints went. "Maybe you should hold the flashlight since you're in front."

"No, I just need to see enough to not run into walls. Too much light will give us away."

Any light would give us away. I craned my neck to see around him. Where was Ted and Lauren? The silence inside the tunnels was deafening. Any scrape of a shoe would be heard with no idea which direction it came from.

There! Exactly what I was thinking...the thud of...a shoe? I gripped Heath's arm.

Another thud. Was someone throwing rocks?

Heath tackled me to the ground. "She can see us. She's shooting with a silencer."

"Oh. Shoot back."

"I don't know where she is." His breath tickled the hair at the nape of my neck. Under normal circumstances, I'd find the position we were in rather...seductive. Right now, I felt safe that he covered me, but worried for him. I wiggled free.

"What do we do?"

"I don't know. I've never been in this predicament before."

"Get out of here!" Ted appeared

around the corner. "She's crazy."

"We came to help you. I promised Grandma." Relief welled in me at the sight of his scowl.

"Get the light out of my face." He shoved my arm down. "You can help by leaving. I don't need to worry about the two of you."

"Any idea where she is?" Heath asked, lifting his gun.

"No, and put the gun away. Is that Ida's? Good grief."

Poor Ted. He must daily regret getting mixed up with my family.

We stood there in silence for what seemed like an eternity. When no sound was forthcoming, we ventured a little further down one of the tunnels.

Ted groaned as we continued to follow him, but I'd made a promise. One I intended to keep. If I returned without him, Grandma wouldn't speak to me for a week.

He held up a hand, stopping us. We listened, then moved on.

"There are several ways out of here," Ted whispered. "I think she's escaped again."

Great. The woman was like a ghost. Here one minute, gone the next. There was no telling where she would show up next.

Ted led us through the tunnels. We emerged next to the maze. "First thing, I want this entrance boarded up," he said. "Once I find the others, I want the same thing done to them. Leave the opening next to the greenhouse for a storm shelter, but close it off a few feet in. No more hide'n go seek with killers."

Heath nodded. "I'll do it first thing in the morning."

I knew what I'd be doing tomorrow. With the damage to trees and bushes from the storm, I'd be taking a page from Alice's book and delegating clean up to the workers in the maze.

"Do you think Lauren killed Teresa?" I asked Ted.

"She's our primary suspect, but I have yet to find a motive."

I nodded. "No one seems to have a motive." I needed to do some deep thinking and some subtle snooping. What I needed now was a clear sign as to where I should snoop.

Ted walked with us as far as my cottage, then headed for Grandma's. We heard her shriek of happiness three doors down.

"Now," Heath put an arm on each side of me, trapping me between him and the door to my place. "I promised you a kiss. Should we do it here in the open or in the privacy of your living room?"

I grabbed his tie and yanked him inside. "No sense in putting on a show."

We pedaled backward. The coffee

table hit me in the back of my knees, felling us to the sofa.

Heath grinned. "This is more like it."

Mom cleared her throat.

I groaned. "How did you get in?"

"Your Grandmother gave me a key." She glared down at us. "I can see what kind of an influence she's been on you."

"Nevertheless. Turn your head, because Heath is going to kiss me in celebration of us getting out of the tunnels alive."

Her frown turned to a smile. "In that case, I'll visit the restroom for three minutes, and three minutes only. Then, we need to talk." She headed down the short hallway.

"Make it three minutes I won't forget." I pulled Heath's face to mine.

I lost all track of time until Mom cleared her throat again. I opened my eyes. "You're like a pall over my happiness."

She shrugged. "Kissing a man who is not your husband for longer than three minutes while lying prone on your back is not wise."

Heath laughed and helped me sit up. "You wanted to talk to us?"

My lips tingled and felt swollen from his kisses. I hadn't wanted to stop. Maybe it had been a good thing Mom was there.

"Well, after the storm," Mom said, sitting across from us, "everyone gathered back in the dining hall for cake. I brought you both a slice and Shelby's gifts. Anyway, conversation flowed like cheap champagne. Especially from the lips of the Poker Boys."

I straightened. "What did they say?"

"It seems William, on his way to visit Teresa, smelled a certain brand of cologne."

Here we went again. I'd found my suspects last time because someone said the killer wore Polo. "And?"

"They didn't recognize the scent, only that it was something heavy and musky and was smelled after a particularly loud argument between the mystery man and Teresa. Most likely it was personally made for the wearer."

"How is that supposed to help?" There had to be hundreds of different colognes.

"You have a nose, don't you? I used mine during the cake eating. Four men wear a scent new to me. Alan, Damon, Harvey, and Scott."

So, Harvey had changed his cologne of choice. I couldn't help but wonder if the scent was one preferred by the woman they all flocked to see. "I need to get into their cottages."

"How do you plan on doing that?" Heath asked. "It isn't like you can knock on their door and waltz through the rooms."

"No, I need a reason for Alice to let me in." If I had a talent for decorating, which I didn't, I could offer my services there. It would be the perfect cover. Maybe I could enter on the pretense of seeing whether anything needed repairing or replaced. I grinned. "I forgot, Alice gave me a master key. I'll start searching during mealtimes."

"People will miss you," Heath said. "You never skip a meal."

"True." I needed spies. People to let me know when one of the suspects left the community for a while. I knew Grandma would be on board. "Mom, I need to know when these four men leave Shady Acres. As receptionist, you see who comes and goes."

"Good, I can help from the safety of my desk." She stood and gave me a hug. "I'll see you at breakfast. Come along, Heath."

He chuckled, gave me a quick kiss,

and followed Mom out the door. The lock clicked.

Alone now, I grabbed a notepad and pencil to jot down some notes.

Lauren tried to kill me and/or Heath, but most likely not Teresa.

Man Teresa argued with wears mystery scent. I listed the four names under that line.

Someone gave Teresa roses shortly before her death. The killer or an admirer?

Motive?

Teresa wanted to be a movie star. She needed money to pursue that dream. She had a "side business".

She left no family, but had...

I was an idiot! I jumped to my feet and raced for my bedroom. Rummaging through my nightstand, I found the envelopes from the roll top desk in Teresa's cottage.

One was a rejection from a talent

scout, another from a modeling agency. The other two looked to be love letters.

I lifted them to my nose, detecting a faint musky cologne. Lifting the flap, I pulled out a sheet of off-white stationary and read:

"Stop threatening me with exposure. I've given you more gifts than a woman of your meager talents deserve." Ouch. "If I wanted a permanent relationship, I wouldn't spend time with a..." I couldn't say the filthy word the writer had called her.

The other letter looked to be written before the nasty one and had the same masculine handwriting.

"Dearest Teresa, your beauty is above the flowers I send you daily. The pearl earrings were nothing compared to the delicacy of your ears." Seriously? Who was this guy? "I cannot wait until our rendezvous. Do you know of the fallen gazebo? Meet me there at ten."

So, the location of her death hadn't been the only time Teresa had gone into the maze. I tapped the pencil I still held against my teeth. If I could find the one who wore this scent and had this handwriting, I would find her killer.

All I needed to do now was find a way to accomplish that. I clicked off the lights and headed to bed.

Grabbing my nightclothes from the bedpost, I stepped into the bathroom. After changing and brushing my teeth, I surveyed the damage to my lovely red dress. Lots of stains, no tears. Hopefully, a good cleaner could restore it. I hung it on the hook on the back of the door, turned off the light and stepped into my bedroom.

A shadow passed by the window.

I froze.

The shadow stopped.

I plastered my back against the wall and slid around the room until I could reach my cell phone where I'd tossed it on the bed. I sent Ted a text message.

Seconds later, my phone rang and the theme to Jurassic Park sent the shadowy figure running. "No worries, Ted, he's gone now."

"Teddy is in the restroom," Grandma said. "I read the text and wanted to make sure you were all right."

"When I send a text like this one, don't call, text me back. You frightened them away."

"You're complaining about the fact I might have scared away someone intending to murder you?"

She had a point. "We might have been able to catch the person."

"Here's Teddy."

"Shelby?"

I explained about the figure outside my window. "I don't think it was an ordinary Peeping Tom." I also told him about the letters and the cologne.

"Why don't you join the police academy and put these skills to legal use?"

"I'm happy doing what I do."

He sighed. "I'll be right over. Stay inside."

In two minutes, a knock sounded on my door. After verifying through the peephole that it was Ted, I opened the door.

"Show me where you saw them?" He flicked on his flashlight.

I led him around the corner to the spot outside my bedroom window. "Those footprints look like a size eleven."

"Okay, Sherlock." He knelt and studied the prints. "You're probably right." Putting his hands on his knees, he pushed to his feet.

"We're getting close. We know the man wears a certain type of cologne, wears a size eleven shoe, and we know what his handwriting looks like."

"I really wish you'd do me a favor and stay out of it."

"You know I have good insight. People talk to me, Ted."

"That's the only reason I haven't thrown you behind bars by now."

15

"*D*amon has left the building." Mom's text came through right after breakfast.

"Time to snoop." I stuck my phone in my pocket and explained to Heath where I was going.

"I'm going with you."

We headed to Damon's cottage. After a cursory look around to make sure no one was paying attention to us, I unlocked the door and we ducked inside. I pulled two pairs of vinyl gloves from my pocket.

"You carry these with you?" Heath snapped them on his hands.

"Better safe than sorry. I'm skating on thin ice with Ted as it is. I don't think he'll turn a blind eye to breaking and entering." I donned my own gloves. "You start in here, I'll start in the bedroom. Look for anything...suspicious or that has to do with Teresa."

Another text from Mom that said, "Alan has left the building."

There may not be time to search both places.

"Scott has left the building."

"Alice has left the building."

"Birdie has left the building."

For crying out loud. I texted back. "Okay, only text me now if Damon returns."

"I found two samples of writing. Do these match the handwriting of the suspect?" Heath handed me an envelope and the residential agreement.

I wasn't a handwriting expert, but they looked like two different people's signatures and didn't match the letter to Teresa. "Snap a pic with your phone."

I headed for the closet. Yep, size eleven loafers. I studied them for signs of recent dirt. Mulch, the type I put in the flower beds was embedded in the shoes. It increased my suspicion, but he could have gotten it anywhere on the grounds.

A search through the clothes hanging there revealed nothing. I stepped out of the closet and checked between the mattresses, under the bed, in the dresser drawers…nada. Zip. Zilch. Other than the mud on his shoes, the man was clean.

"Found something!" Heath called from the other room.

I rushed to his side or rather the counter he stood on. He handed me a cookie jar that looked like a monkey.

Inside was diamonds. Lots of loose diamonds and other precious stones. "Well, he is a retired jeweler. Maybe he still makes jewelry."

Heath held out his hand for the jar. "A bit risky. Wouldn't they be safer in a deposit box somewhere?"

It was odd, but not something to cause alarm. "Take a picture." I texted Mom, found out Alan was still gone, so we headed next door.

The cottage looked as if no one lived there. No books or magazines on the coffee table. No dishes in the sink. Every sofa pillow plumped to perfection and in its place. Even the laptop sat precisely on the dinette table, nothing but a Cross ink pen beside it.

In my opinion, only crazy people lived like this. There were still vacuum tracks in the carpet. How were we going to enter without his knowing?

"This will be tough," Heath said. "I can't even vacuum behind us and put the vacuum back where it belongs."

"So what do we do?"

"We can stay in his prints, but it limits

where we look."

"It's all we've got." I placed my foot in Alan's size eleven print and followed them to the bedroom.

Thank goodness there were no vaccum tracks here. I again headed for the closet first. Of course it was meticulous. Clothes were hung according to use and color. Something was seriously wrong with this man.

No mud on his shoes, of course. But I did find signs he'd scraped them on a nearby trashcan. Bingo. Black boxes lined the top shelf, full of receipts and other important documents. Nothing that looked as if it were to or from Teresa, though.

I checked the other usual places until my cell phone dinged signally a text. "Albatross returning."

What the heck? I hope she meant Alan. "Gotta go, Heath!"

I quickly retraced my steps, pausing at

the front door to take one last look around.

"May I help you?" I turned and stared into the curious expression of Alan. "Just checking to see whether anything needs replaced or repaired."

"I hope you didn't go inside. I just vacuumed."

"Nope. Just got the door unlocked and you showed up."

"Good. I'm just fine. Nothing to concern yourselves with." He gave a stiff smile and entered his cottage.

"Pleasant guy," Heath said.

"Facetious much?"

He laughed and gave me a quick one-armed hug. "Why don't you check to see whether Scott is still out?"

He was, so we made that our next stop. His cottage couldn't be more different than Alan's. This was a single man's hovel for sure.

There wasn't a square inch not

covered with something. "We'll have to hurry. This will take a while."

I totally scored in a box under the bed. Inside were photos of Teresa and the shadowy forms of men entering her cottage. There were also letters with the suspect's signature. Buried under the papers was a ruby ring I would have died to possess. I snapped pics of everything and shoved it under the bed.

"Uh, Shelby?" Heath stood in the doorway.

Behind him, clutching a pistol which was aimed at Heath's head, was Scott. "Mind telling me why the two of you are snooping in my cottage?"

"Oh, uh...we were checking to see if anything needs repairing or replaced." I forced a smile. "No need for violence. We can go."

Scott sighed and lowered the gun. "I think the three of us need to have a conversation. Sit in the living room please."

Without arguing, we followed orders. Once we sat, Heath took my hand in his and squeezed. "It'll be fine."

I nodded.

Scott sat across from us, laying the gun on the side table next to him. "I guess I have some explaining to do."

"You can start with why you killed Teresa," I said.

"What? I didn't kill Teresa. I loved her, still do." Sorrow shadowed his face.

"Then why the gun?"

"Someone has been leaving me threatening notes."

"Can we quit with the twenty questions and you tell us what's going on?" Heath leaned forward. "I don't take you for a killer."

"I'm not. The gun isn't even loaded." He shook his head and dangled his hands between his knees. "As soon as I got the job helping you as hired hand, I started my own investigation into Teresa's death."

"Surely you've heard that's what we're doing?" I frowned. "Why not approach us?"

"I don't know who to trust."

"Haven't you seen Officer Lawrence with us? He shadows our every move. That ought to show you can trust us. Have you caught anyone looking in your windows?"

"Yeah. It's the old lady Wilkinson. She's harmless."

I'd seen her around, but haven't met her. With the way Alice kept me running there were several of the quieter residents I had yet to meet. Still, I doubted the woman wore a size eleven in men's shoes.

"You've spoken to her?"

"After I caught her peeking. She's a bit of a perv, but it's kind of funny, don't you think?"

"Not really. Did you learn anything?"

It was clear he wasn't sure whether to trust us or not. He stared at me for a moment, then at Heath before shrugging. "She said Teresa fought with the same man every night but she didn't know his name. Only that he was a resident here."

"All she would have to do is ask."

"She doesn't like people."

I raised my eyebrows. Heath and I needed to pay the little old woman a visit. "Didn't it bother you how she earned most of her money?"

His head snapped up. "Of course it did. We had our own arguments about it."

"That's a good motive for murder."

"I wouldn't have hurt her. Ever." He seemed sincere.

"Who do you think killed Teresa?"

"I can't tell you that. Not until I'm sure." He stood. "I'm sure you understand. If I make an accusation, that puts me in more danger. I'll see you out."

I called Mom to have her look up Ms. Wilkinson's cottage number, then Heath and I headed right to number twenty-two. She answered the door in a snap up the front house dress, rollers in her hair, and a cigarette dangling from her lips. The glare in her eyes told me she wasn't going to be friendly. Her words confirmed it.

"What do you want?"

"I...uh..." needed to learn how to be a better liar, if truth be told. "Do you have any repairs or replacements that need done in your cottage?"

"That's the lamest thing I've ever heard. I saw you come from that Scott boy's place. Not much misses my eyes, girlie. Come on in and ask your stupid questions."

We entered a cottage decorated like the 1950s. She'd even painted her kitchen appliances pink. Alice would have a fit if she knew.

"If you're going to ask me who killed that girl, I don't know. She kept her curtains closed up tight. As if that would hide her dirty secrets." She cackled and blew smoke through her nose.

"You must know something." I perched on a floral sofa covered in plastic. "I've heard you make the rounds."

"Looking in windows, you mean. Say what you mean, girl. I'm not one to mince words."

I didn't guess she was. Deciding to adopt a practice of Ted's, I kept my mouth closed and just looked at her.

Heath perched next to me, his lips twitching as he tried to hide his amusement.

"Don't laugh, boy. I've seen that crazy decorating woman hanging around your place."

His humor faded. "That's in the past."

"Is it? I saw her just last night roaming around your cottage trying to find a way inside."

Heath glanced at me, then back at our smoking hostess. "Why didn't you call the police?"

"I thought you wanted her there."

"No. She tried to kill me."

"Oh, well." She stubbed out her cigarette and lit another. "The person you ought to be asking questions of is that vampire man. I've heard he can walk through walls."

"I've already spoken to Leroy." I turned my head to avoid the smoke.

"Sorry if you don't like my smoke," she said. "But it is my house."

"I'm not complaining." I coughed. "Is there nothing you can tell us?"

"I can tell you a lot. The man has grey hair and average size feet. Husky voice and wears a musky cologne."

Things we already knew except for the grey hair. Most of the male population of Shady Acres had grey hair. Discouragement choked me as much as the second hand smoke.

"We'll be leaving you. Be careful, Ms. Wilkinson and stop peeping in windows. It isn't safe."

"It amuses me. Why would you want to take away an old woman's fun. See yourselves out." She waved a hand. "I'll let you know if I see anything of importance."

We thanked her and stepped outside. "Another day wasted where I could be working on the tornado damage."

Heath patted my shoulder. "We're getting closer, I can feel it. She knows more than she's saying."

"Which could be very dangerous for her."

Something banged the side of the cottage.

We darted around the corner in time to see a man in a black hoodie race for the trees.

We took chase, me pulling my Tazor out of my pocket. I wasn't chasing anyone without some kind of weapon in my hand.

The man lost us as soon as he crossed the treeline.

"That's unfortunate," I said.

"Especially for Ms. Wilkinson. Call Ted. I'm pretty sure that man heard our conversation. He'll be back to make sure she doesn't talk."

16

"I ought to rent a cottage here," Ted said when he arrived after our call.

"No vacancies," I grinned.

"I wasn't serious." He knocked on Ms. Wilkinson's door.

She yanked it open with a scowl. "Figured they'd rat me out. Come on in."

Since Ted shook his head at our entering with him, Heath and I went to the next cottage on our list. Leroy's. It was a bit early in the day for our resident vampire, not that he was really a vampire, only had a severe reaction to sunlight, but I figured if we knocked hard enough we could wake him up.

He was up. "Shelby! Come on in. Welcome, Heath."

"Good morning, Leroy." Heath let me enter first and we sat at the dinette table while our host poured us a cup of coffee.

"What brings you two to my humble abode when I'm usually sleeping?" Leroy sat across from us.

"We've been snooping and asking questions," I said with a smile. "Also, you wouldn't happen to know anyone with a size eleven shoe that might be peeking in my windows, do you?"

"That would be me."

"What? Why?" I'd never taken him for a pervert before.

He sighed. "I worry about you, Shelby. Of course, I'm going to be watching."

"Thank you, Leroy," Heath said. "I feel better knowing you've got an eye on her."

"It's an invasion of privacy!" I plopped

my cup on the table. "Just knock on the door like a regular human."

"But I'm not a regular human. Haven't you heard? I'm the prince of darkness."

"It isn't funny. You scared me."

"That I do apologize for."

He certainly didn't look sorry. Instead, I rather felt as if he were patronizing me. I also was no longer sure whether our suspect wore a size eleven shoe. All we knew with fair certainty was that the killer was a grey-haired male.

"Don't look so despondent, Shelby," Leroy said. "You'll catch the killer."

"He'll most likely find me first. Just like last time." Lord, don't let me be locked in a burning building again.

"Maybe it's time for you to confront your suspects. Flush 'em out, so to speak."

"Don't encourage her, Leroy," Heath said. "Nosing around, then passing the information to Ted, is the safest thing to do."

"Whatever happened to that Lauren gal?"

"She's disappeared."

I decided to focus on my slightly bitter coffee and let the men discuss how I should live my life. Or not live it if my luck ran out.

My cell phone buzzed. It was Alice wondering where we were and why we weren't supervising the workers who were on yet another break.

"We have to get to work. Let us know if you see anything, Leroy." I gathered our cups and set them in his sink.

"Will do. Be safe."

Heath headed to the boathouse while I made my way to the maze. Sure enough, the four workers I'd hired were sitting under a shade tree having a conversation.

"What's up, gentlemen?" I stared down where they lounged on the grass.

"There's something in the maze you should see." The leader of the group, Rob, got to his feet. "Maybe you should give us your cell number so we can reach you when we need to.

Good point. I gave him my number and followed him into the maze. They'd made a lot of progress over the last few days, putting up sheets of plywood where the tornado ripped out pieces of the maze. It wasn't as pretty, but I knew the hedge would grow back.

He led me down a path lined with sticks sporting ribbons until we got to the gazebo, or at least where the gazebo once stood. Now, it resembled little more than a pile of weathered wood.

"That's a shame." I put my hands on my hips. "Can you rebuild?"

"Yes, ma'am. But, that isn't what I brought you here to see." He led me around the back of the pile.

Sticking out of the dirt was a small

ornate box. I squatted in front of it, wanting to pull it out of its resting spot, but knowing Ted would kill me. Wait. What if it had nothing to do with the murder?

I tugged on it until it came free. Drat. Locked. I was sure Heath could get it open. "Thanks. The maze is looking great."

"We thought we'd be finished by the weekend, but building the gazebo back will take longer. Want us to string lights? We can have them operate off a battery."

"That would be wonderful." And so pretty at night time. I made a mental note to have the maze activity one week from this weekend.

Clutching the box to my chest, I left the maze, told the workers to get back to work, and headed for my cottage. I needed a safe place to hide the box until I had time to open it. The closet and under the bed were too common.

I shoved the box in the broiler part of the oven with my baking pans. It should be safe enough there.

Confident no one would find the box, I headed for the toolshed and my wheelbarrow. It had been too long since I'd gotten my hands dirty and there were weeds to be pulled. Not to mention new flowers that were delivered the day before. If not for Alice's demands, and trying to find Teresa's killer, I'd be digging in the dirt every hour of my working day.

As I dug, I again went over what I knew about Teresa's killer...which wasn't much. Maybe Leroy was right. I needed to confront my suspects. Lauren, since she was in hiding, was out. That left...half the population of Shady Acres.

Who were the more womanizing men there? The Poker Boys, of course, but they weren't killers. That left Alan Barker and Damon Markson. My questioning them would be a wonderful welcome to the community. They'd probably move, then Alice would have my head. Residents were already dropping like flies since my arrival.

I stood and popped the kinks from my back. Headed for the pool, a towel over his shoulder, and wearing of all things a speedo, was Damon. Gross. Still, I put my tools in the wheelbarrow and followed.

Since the man was a huge flirt, he shouldn't need much encouragement to talk. I wheeled into the pool area and started trimming nearby bushes.

"There's the belle of Shady Acres." Damon's voice rang out.

And, so it begins.

"I'm looking for some new arm candy. Want the job?" He leaned against the pool side and grinned over his shoulder.

Gag. "I'm with Heath, but thank you for the compliment." I snipped a branch as if it were his neck. "Too bad Teresa isn't here. She would have jumped at the chance."

"Yeah, sad what happened to her. She was a looker. She wouldn't have been the one for me, though. I like my women focused on me, not enjoying the company of other men."

Understandable. I made a noncommittal noise and kept snipping.

"You know, though, a woman's place is next to her man. Not dozens of others. A woman needs to choose."

I glared at the back of his head. "I suppose it's different for men?"

"Yes. It has been since the beginning of time."

I made a sniffing motion at his neck. "If you say so."

He glanced back. "You don't agree?"

"I don't believe in double standards."

"I could convince you." He sneered.

"No, thanks." I needed a shower just

from talking to him. "I'd best move on."

"A gorgeous woman like you shouldn't be doing manual labor. You should be reclining amongst luxury."

"We can all dream." I let the pool gate slam behind me and rolled the wheelbarrow over Alan's bare feet.

He cursed and jumped back. "Careless woman."

This one wasn't as flirtatious as the one in the water. "I'm so sorry."

"I guess you were thinking on the true words of Mr. Markson."

"You agree with him?" How many chauvinists did this place have? One was too many.

"Without a doubt." He shoved past me and limped inside.

I spotted Heath coming my way. I motioned for him to come with me to the toolshed. Once there, I explained about the box the workers had found.

"Let's go take a look. The boathouse

is coming along nicely. Should be finished in a day or two. I was on my way to tell Alice to order the boats and kayaks, but that can wait."

We hurried to my cottage and retrieved the box from its hiding place. Heath had the lock cut off in a matter of minutes.

"This is exciting!"

He smiled. "Hopefully something good is inside."

Like children opening a Christmas present, we peered in as Heath slowly peeled back the lid. Nestled inside were false teeth, a watch, prescription bottles with Bob's name on them, and a necklace. Maybelle's treasures.

My first day on the job I'd found Maybelle's body in the greenhouse. She'd been poisoned under the orchids. Well, accidentally, as she'd ingested the poison intended for Alice. I'd always wondered where some of her stolen things had gone.

"Let's give this to Alice." Heath closed the box and stuffed it under his arm.

Alice was supervising the dinner buffet when we found her. "I hope you two are working and not spending all your time investigating. Officer Lawrence is here enough to do that himself."

"The workers found this in the maze." Heath handed her the box.

"It's some of the things Maybelle had stolen."

She raised wide eyes to us. "Talk about old things coming back to haunt you. That isn't the only thing reappearing. Take a look at the women's mirror in the bathroom."

Lauren was back? I dashed into the bathroom, Heath on my heels despite Alice's protests.

The message simply stated, "Bang."

I guess our game wasn't over.

"I don't like this," Heath said. He

grabbed a paper towel and smeared the message. "Don't answer back."

"Where is she hiding? If she can get here to do this, she can't be far." I had no intention of answering, but he'd made a mess on the mirror that I would have to clean up.

Just as I headed for glass cleaner, sirens filled the air. I took one look at Heath and Alice and sprinted for the door. The sirens grew louder.

We barged outside as Ted, gun drawn, raced toward the cottages. We followed at a run.

The ambulance stopped in front of Ms. Wilkinson's.

"Stay back." Ted gave us a stern look. "I don't need anyone in the way."

"What happened?" Tears filled my eyes.

"We got a 911 call about an intruder. Stay behind the sidewalk, please."

We did as ordered and waited, my

heart in my throat, for some word. It took fifteen minutes to come out.

"No one in there except Ms. Wilkinson. I'm sorry to tell you, she's dead. Obvious cause of death is strangulation with a red scarf."

I put a hand over my mouth. "We just spoke to her this morning."

"I'll need to know about that conversation when I'm through here."

Heath drew me into his arms. "Someone heard our conversation. This is getting bad."

"We need to find out where everyone was at the time of death," Alice said, writing something on her clipboard. "I'll make an announcement for everyone to return to their cottages."

"Good idea," Ted said. "No one leaves until I've spoken with them."

She hurried off. Moments later, we heard, "There has been a situation at Shady Acres. All residents return to their cottages and stay until further notice."

Nothing like frightening the masses. Like a herd of frightened cattle, the dining room emptied and folks headed home.

"That's efficient." Ted re-entered the cottage.

"Can I come in?"

"Shelby, I'll let you in after my investigators are finished. I know you have a good eye, but you don't need to see this."

Sadness over another death filled my heart. I wiped my tears on my dirty arm and turned to lay my head on Heath's chest. I vowed to find the killer by the maze event.

17

*A*fter three hours, Ms. Wilkinson's body was removed from her cottage. I really wanted to follow Ted door-to-door, but curiosity had me entering the crime scene instead.

There might not have been blood often associated with a violent death, but the chair and coffee table were overturned. The bulb of a lamp shattered. A struggle had ensued. I really hoped she had put up a good fight.

I blinked away the tears stinging my eyes and wandered through the cottage. Other than the front room, nothing seemed amiss. Most likely, her assailant had knocked on the door and she'd let him in.

Had she been strangled with her own scarf or had the killer brought it with him? "There's nothing to see here."

"If she fought, the killer might be sporting some scratches." Heath put his arm around my shoulder. "We'll check the guests once everyone is released from their cottages. They'll most likely congregate in the dining hall to compare notes."

"You're right." It would be the best place to gather clues. For now, we'd have to go with my first idea and shadow Ted.

We located him at Bob's where the Poker Boys had gathered following Alice's announcement. While the cottage door was closed, the window was open. Unembarassed at stooping to eavesdropping, I planted myself within clear hearing distance.

"We were at lunch," Bob said. "You can find plenty of people to attest to that."

"Anyone not at lunch?"

"Shelby and Heath weren't there. Neither was Ms. Wilkinson, that Damon fella, or Alan Barker." He paused. "Alice wasn't there at first. She came in late. Let me think...yeah, Scott was missing, but that isn't unusual. The boy stays to himself a lot. Oh, and Leroy, but he's never at the meals."

"Most people attend the meals fairly regularly," William said. "It's social time. It was strange that Shelby wasn't there. She might be a little thing, but she puts away some food."

I smiled. My friends were awesome, if not exactly moral.

"We're done here. You men are free to leave," Ted said.

"You don't suspect us?" Bob asked.

"No, sir."

"Then we aren't doing something right." He laughed, the others joining in.

The front door to the cottage opened. Ted stepped around the corner of the cottage and glared. "Shelby, you're a trial."

"I'm not breaking any laws or getting in your way."

A look of exasperation appeared on his face. "Good." He marched to the next cottage, which happened to be Mom's.

"You don't need to bother her. She isn't a killer." I jogged to catch up with him.

"She might have seen something. I'm not leaving anyone out."

He tried to shut the door in my face when Mom opened it, but I stuck my foot in the way. "She's my mother."

"Seriously, Ted." Mom gave him 'that look' and ushered me and Heath inside.

Ted groaned. "I think it's time to retire."

"Well, Minerva's cottage will be available soon," Grandma said from her spot on the sofa. "I know that is crude and crass at this time, but it's the truth. You want to move to Shady Acres, now is the time."

Sometimes, I could not believe the words that came out of her mouth. "Really, Grandma." I plopped next to her on the sofa.

"What?" She looked at me in astonishment. "I'm only stating a fact." Transferring her attention back to Ted, she said, "I was here with Sue Ellen and didn't see a thing."

"It's true," Mom said, averting her gaze. A true tell that she was lying.

"Then how do the two of you know what happened?" Ted narrowed his eyes.

"I have failed to teach Sue Ellen how to tell a white lie," Grandma said. "We did see something, but wanted to let

Shelby know first. People tend to clam up when you're around Teddy."

"That's impeding my investigation, Ida."

"I apologize for that. Very well, since Shelby is here...now, I'm not accusing anyone, but I saw a man in a black hoodie knocking on Minerva's door. She opened it and told him to go away, but then seemed to reconsider and let him in."

"You didn't see his face?" Ted's pen scratched furiously across his notepad.

"He has a big nose. That's all that I could see with his hood up. Oh, and he was Caucasian, as the cops say."

A big nose could be anyone or a few, depending on who Grandma thought fit that description. I'd be studying faces at the next meal. We were getting close. I could feel it. I could also tell from the expression on Ted's face that he had a suspect in mind. Getting the name from him would be quite the task.

"What do you consider a big nose?" Ted asked.

"Maybe it wasn't big, but that's all I could see."

And my only clue flew out the window.

"So, all you can say with certainty is that is was a white male?" Ted asked.

Grandma nodded. "Yes, I can say that with certainty."

"Sue Ellen?"

"That's what she told me."

Ted nodded. "You saw nothing on your own?"

"No, I popped in here to grab a book to read while sitting at the reception desk. When Alice made her announcement, my mother came here. She said it wasn't safe for old women to be alone."

Ted's head jerked back to Grandma. "You knew there had been a murder?"

"Why else would Alice make such a statement? I've been around long enough to know that death lives at Shady Acres. This place is deliciously cursed."

"It is not." Just because I'd found a body on my first day, which so happened to be Grandma's first day, and then two more bodies since then, three counting Ms. Wilkinson, didn't mean the place was cursed.

I liked it here, despite the murders. We were a community of fifty residents and many employees. There were bound to be a few dramatic upsets, right? Or maybe I was plain bad luck.

"I have all I need here. You ladies are free to leave the cottage." Ted slipped his notepad in his pocket.

"There are two murderers out there, Teddy!" Grandma's eyes widened. "Lauren and the unknown man. Why would you send us out there?"

"Then stay here." He shrugged. "If

you women didn't snoop around, you wouldn't be in danger."

"In their defense," Heath spoke up, "they can't help themselves. And, Lauren, is after me."

"And me." I raised my hand.

"Fine, stay in or go out. I have work to do." Ted stormed from the cottage with me and Heath on his heels.

"Mrs. Wilkinson wasn't a danger to anyone," I said, catching up to him. "All she knew was that the man who argued with Teresa had grey hair. That's most of the men here. So, why did the killer go after her? If it was Teresa's sugar daddy, Ms. Wilkinson didn't fit the type of woman he would spend time with."

"Heath said something about a conversation the two of you had?"

"Which only said the man had grey hair."

"She must have known something else. The woman was a snoop, like someone else I know."

It was possible she'd withheld information from me, but why? She'd seemed quite forthcoming during my visit. I supposed she could have discovered something else in the short time since I'd seen her. "It doesn't make sense."

"Her killer must have thought she knew more than she did."

Been there, done that.

Ted groaned. "Why is he roaming the grounds?"

I followed the direction he looked. Scott stood in the middle of the sidewalk, glancing around the area. He looked confused.

"Scott!"

He jogged toward us. "Where is everyone?"

"Didn't you hear the announcement?"

"No, I ran out to get some paint to

touch up the door frames in the main building."

"There's been a murder," Ted said. "Can someone vouch that you were where you were?"

"I suppose the clerk could." He rubbed his hand.

"Where did you get the scratches, sir?" Ted reached for his handcuffs.

"There's a sharp edge on the door of my truck. I had a slight accident a year ago, and it's rusty." Scott glanced from me to him to Heath. "Heath has mentioned I should fix it several times."

"That's true." Heath nodded.

Ted relaxed his posture, but the hard glint in his eyes should have made Scott fear for his life. "Don't leave the grounds until I get to the bottom of this."

"Yes, sir. I'll go straight to my cottage." He dashed away.

Our next stop was Alan Barker's. He wasn't home. Neither was Damon

Markson. Very interesting.

"Any idea where these two men are?"

I shook my head. "They leave a lot. I think they have girlfriends living in town."

"I hope they have alibis."

Ah ha! "You suspect one of them."

He cut me a glance. "I suspect every grey haired man at this point."

"Even yourself?" I grinned.

"Very funny. Why don't the two of you make yourselves useful and go write down everything you know about the men who live here."

"Sure." Grateful to have something constructive to do, I headed to my place with Heath.

Once there, I got out my suspect list. "I've narrowed it down to Alan and Damon."

"Why?" Heath peered over my shoulder.

"A gut feeling. Scott may have

scratches, but he didn't kill anyone. I'd stake my life on it."

"You might have to if you're wrong."

"Both of these men flit around here like ghosts. They come and go at all hours. They're both the type to have visited Teresa, especially Damon. He's a snake. They have grey hair. What we needed to do was get into their cottages and search for a black hoodie.

18

I wasn't keen on visiting Alan's and Damon's cottages again, but there didn't seem to be any other way. The only time to do so with any degree of safety, was when they were gone or at dinner.

I opted for dinner. If I kept skipping too many of the meals in the dining hall, people were going to talk and, possibly, start coming to look for me. Especially when the main reason lately for someone not showing was because they were dead.

I shed my rain boots, they were hard to run in, and donned a pair of gym shoes. Then, grabbing a pair of gloves and a flashlight, I left my cottage, locking the door behind me.

"Where are you going?" Heath leaned against the wall. "Trying to snoop on your own?"

"I'd planned on it. But, now that that isn't an option, you can be my lookout."

"Where are you going?"

"Alan's and Damon's. I want to know whether they have black hoodies." I swung my key ring around my finger.

"I have a black hoodie, Shelby."

I stopped and glared up at him. "But you aren't a killer, or even a suspect. These two are. There's a big difference."

He mumbled something about reckless women, but wisely changed the subject. Sort of. "Why not let Ted handle things?"

"Because I've discovered I have a talent for solving murders." I grinned. I did, sort of. I mean, Cheryl and I had caught Maybelle's killer. Well, we'd discovered it was him moments before he locked us in a shed and set fire to it, so that counted in my book.

As we approached Alan's cottage, Heath grabbed my arm and yanked me around the corner. "He's just now leaving for dinner."

That could have been very awkward. I needed a new story to tell if we were caught. Better yet, don't get caught. "We need a signal."

Heath nodded. "One whistle, like a bird's call, if someone is coming. I'll whistle a jaunty tune if it's Alan heading for the cottage."

"Great idea."

Once Alan had entered the dining hall, I took another look around, then unlocked his front door and slipped inside, leaving Heath to pretend he was fixing some trim around one of the windows.

Inside, I headed once again for the closet. If the man owned a hoodie, it would be there, in a drawer, or in a clothes hamper. I sincerely hoped it wasn't in the clothes hamper. Digging through a man's dirty underwear wasn't on my list of pleasant ways to spend an evening.

But, that's exactly what I ended up doing. I was picking through an overflowing pile of dirty laundry, when I heard Heath whistle a jaunty tune from Snow White.

I spotted a black hoodie and lifted it. Dirt covered the front of the item. By then, Heath's whistle had gotten louder and faster. There'd be no escaping out the front door.

Dropping the hoodie, I raced for the bedroom window and flung it open as the front door closed. I dove through, landing in a rosebush that needed a good trimming, then lowered the window and scooted around the corner.

My chest heaved as I fought to slow my breathing. I was certain Alan could hear it through the wall of his bedroom. When no angry shout came out the window, I darted to where Heath waited.

"That was close." He gripped my shoulders. "Did he see you?"

"No, and he has a very dirty hoodie in his hamper. Why did he come back?"

"He brought a plate of food with him. I haven't seen Damon come out though."

The search of Damon's cottage was fruitless. No black hoodie. That shot Alan to the top of my suspect list, but didn't necessarily mean he was our guy. Black hoodies were a very popular clothes item. They just weren't usually worn during summer in Arkansas. The very thought made sweat bead on my upper lip.

"I'm going to grab something from the buffet and take it home to eat. It's been a long day."

"I'll come with you, if you don't mind the company."

I smiled. "I never mind your company." In fact, as time went by, I found myself craving his company. The more, the better.

Plates full of fried chicken and potato salad, Southern food night must be the theme, we headed for my cottage. Once we were seated at the dinette, talk turned at once to the murders.

"We don't know for sure that the man in the black hoodie is the killer," Heath said, "but it's our best guess at this point."

"Alan shot to the top of my list." I forked potato salad into my mouth. Yuck. Miracle Whip instead of mayonnaise. "But, he's only there for lack of anyone better."

"We know the motive for Ms. Wilkinson," Heath said. "She knew too much and was talking. But with Teresa...I can't come up with a solid motive. It was no secret what she did for money after hours. Maybe one of her friends did a little too much pillow talk and needed to make sure she didn't repeat anything."

"Makes sense to me." I sat back in my chair. "In fact, it's the best motive so far. Like Ms. Wilkinson, Teresa must have known too much about something."

"The trick will be in finding what these two women might have known, outside of their killer's identity. Find the motive...find the killer."

"How simple." I laughed and collected the dishes to be returned to the dining hall. "I'll carry these if you'll carry my garbage."

"Deal." Heath tied the bag in my kitchen garbage and followed me outside.

Heath leaned over the dumpster behind the main building. "Hold on." He dropped the bag of trash outside the dumpster and climbed inside.

"What are you doing?" Was there anything grosser than a community garbage?

"Found something." He tossed a black hoodie over the side and climbed out. "Alan most likely isn't our killer, unless he threw this away recently."

Using two fingers, I held up the hoodie. "Nope. This one doesn't have dirt smeared across the front. It isn't Alan's. We need to get this to Ted right away."

Heath tossed the bag of garbage into the dumpster while I dialed Ted.

"Please don't tell me you found another body."

"Nope. A black hoodie in the garbage."

"On my way. Don't touch it."

Ooops. Too late.

I carried the dirty dishes to the dining

hall and placed them on the sideboard intended for that purpose while Heath waited outside for Ted. The officer was already there when I returned and putting the hoodie into a bag.

"You must have been at Grandma's."

"I was. So, did you touch this?"

"We both did," Heath said. "I fished it out of the dumpster, and Shelby verified whether it was like the one we found in Alan's cottage."

Ted narrowed his eyes. "Don't tell me how you know what clothing Alan Barker has."

"Okay." I grinned. "Shall Heath tell you instead?"

"No." He marched away with the bag and headed for the parking lot.

Poor Ted. I had to be the proverbial thorn in his side. I couldn't help but feel a bit of pride over that fact.

I turned to Heath. "Now what?"

"Let's walk and come up with what

Teresa might have known about someone. If we come up with something good, maybe it will make the killer stand out a bit more."

"Don't forget I intend to outright question our suspects."

"I wish you wouldn't." He took my hand and led me toward the garden. "But, if you insist, then I'll have to be with you."

"They'll talk more if I'm alone."

"Not happening."

I tugged him to a stop. "Get one of those two-way ear thingies. You can hear the conversation and barge to the rescue if I need you."

"When do you plan on doing this?"

"Tomorrow." I had no intentions of interviewing a possible murderer at night. "Maybe in the dining hall. I'd be really safe there. Alan and Damon usually eat alone."

"Yeah, they don't like the older

women much."

"I bet they did know Teresa, and knew her in the biblical sense. Maybe that's why they moved to Shady Acres. What if they wanted to keep an eye on her?"

"Both of them?"

"Whichever one of them is the killer."

"Maybe." He sat on a carved cement bench. "We know that Teresa read gossip magazines and wanted to move to Hollywood. While working as Shady Acres's receptionist, she also worked as a lady of the evening. Her cottage was full of expensive clothes and jewelry. Am I forgetting anything?"

"I wonder where all her money is." I ran my hand down a pair of capris that had once belonged to Teresa.

"The bank most likely."

"Wouldn't that raise a red flag? I mean, with all the customers she had, she had to be making enough that someone would question that type of a salary for a receptionist."

"Do you think she hid the cash at Shady Acres?" Heath glanced around. "Where would it be safe?"

"The maze. Just like Maybelle had done."

"Let me get a flashlight."

"Get the one out of the shed. It's closer." I handed him my keys.

"I have a set. " He winked and jogged off, then apparently remembering I'd be sitting alone, in the dark, came back and had me go with him.

Soon, we were entering the very dark maze. The workers had finished and the hedges were well trimmed and eight feet tall. I'd caught a glimpse of the gazebo before they left and it would shine like a beacon when lit.

We shined our lights along the path, looking for anything disturbed. I didn't think the money, if it was here, would be in the hedges. If so, the workmen would have found it. I decided to concentrate on benches placed in various locations and large rocks that could be used to hide the signs of digging.

"I'm going right," Heath said. "You go left. Yell if you run across anything."

"Okay." I turned and moseyed down the path, my gaze trained on the ground. Frustrated at what could very well be a wasted couple of hours, I plopped onto a bench and swerved my flashlight beam back and forth.

Wait. A rock different from the rest, as in not covered with a fine layer of clay dust, beckoned to me with its cleanliness. Yep, someone had definitely cleaned the rock to make it stand out. I rolled it out of the way. My beam landed on a metal box. The kind you might keep your yard sale change in.

"Heath!" I hoped he would be able to hear me. I didn't want to be alone in the maze with a ton of money and a killer who might want that money. "Heath!"

"I'm here." He jogged toward me. "Find something."

I placed the box on the bench and opened the lid. There had to be hundreds, if not thousands, of dollars inside. "Do you think she was coming here to retrieve this when she was killed?"

"No, I think your first assumption was correct. She had a rendezvous with her killer. Let's take this to Ted." Heath closed the lid and slipped the box under his arm.

Taking the chance Ted had returned to Grandma's after leaving Shady Acres, we headed there and walked in.

"You should lock your door, Grandma." I frowned. "Is Ted here?"

"In the little boy's room. There's no need for me to worry about anything when my armed man is around."

Speaking of armed man, Ted came out of the bathroom in nothing but his boxers. He cursed and dashed back in when he spotted us. "You could have warned me, Ida!"

"Where's the fun in that?" She giggled. "So." She rubbed her hands together. "What's in the box?"

"Teresa's money, we think." Heath set the box on the coffee table.

"Where did you find it?"

"The maze."

"What made you think to look for hidden money?" Ted, now decently clothed in a pair of jeans and a tee-shirt rejoined us.

"We were brainstorming," I said. "Trying to come up with a motive for her murder."

"If you had a brain, I might believe that." He gave me a hint of a smile and stared at the box. "I doubt the killer's prints are on it, but it won't hurt to look.

I'll take this to the station. You two did a good job."

"Wow. A true miracle." Things were definitely looking up if Ted could pay me a compliment after I'd seen him in his shorts.

19

There was no other way to do things than outright. I sat across the table from Alan Barker and Damon Markson. Both men wore smirks on their faces. I wanted to slap them, and I hadn't asked any questions yet.

"So, did either of you know Teresa Givens?"

Alan chuckled. "What is this an inquisition? A lot of men in town knew the girl, if you know what I mean."

I did, and the thought disgusted me. "Well?"

"I knew her," Alan said.

"So did I," Damon added. "Why are you asking?" He winked. "Are you thinking of taking her place?"

Gross. "I've been asked by the authorities to help solve her murder." Not really, but they wouldn't know that, would they?

"Isn't that dangerous for a civilian? Especially a little thing like you." Damon crossed his arms. "Are we the only ones you're questioning or are you making the rounds?"

I thought I was the one asking questions. "Everyone with grey hair. A witness said a man in a black hoodie was seen leaving a victim's cottage and another said the man had grey hair."

Alan's eyes hardened. "I'm having trouble believing Officer Lawrence, who has already questioned everyone, by the way, is letting you interfere."

"Who said anything about interfering? I'm helping." I glanced at

Damon's hands. Three long red marks marred the surface. "Where did you get the scratches?"

"Working on my car."

The men stood. That's when I noticed scratches along Alan's neck. Very interesting. "Well, the police are doing testing on the skin beneath the latest victim's nails. We'll know soon enough."

"Don't help too much, girlie. That's how little ones get hurt." Alan motioned for Damon to follow him.

That didn't give me any new information. I wanted to throw my pencil at them. Instead, I got up and sat down at the table where Scott sat alone. The poor guy looked as if he'd lost his puppy.

"What's wrong?"

He glanced up from under lowered lashes. "I'm getting nowhere on this case. I've learned Teresa wasn't the girl I thought she was. Because of...what she did for money, no one seems inclined to help me."

"I'm helping you."

Hope sprang to his face. "Have you learned anything?"

"A bit." I wasn't sure how much to tell him. While I didn't think he was a killer, I'd been wrong before and almost died because of it. "Do you have a grey-haired wig?"

"Huh?" His brow lowered.

"Nevermind. The killer may have grey hair."

"Great." He slapped the table. "That's all the men here except for Heath and I. Anything else?"

"He may have worn a black hoodie."

"I own a black hoodie! You aren't helping."

I shrugged. "I'm doing my best. The conclusions I've drawn are one, the killer thought Teresa knew too much about something she shouldn't, or two, he wanted to know where she hid her money."

"You found her money in the maze?"

I narrowed my eyes. "How did you know?"

"I put it there. She said it was her life savings and she didn't trust banks." He covered his face with his hands. "I'm a fool for loving such a woman."

"Men throughout history have been taken for a fool by a beautiful woman. You're one of many." I patted his hand. "Let me know if you do find out anything."

"Sure, but I'm not much of a detective."

Poor thing. Well, I could only hope to find justice for him. Wait a minute. Damon gave me the impression a moment ago that he knew Teresa, but at the pool a few days ago, he said he'd never met her. Lying scum.

"Where are you going in such a tizzy?" Grandma stepped in front of me.

I explained about Damon. "I intend to confront him in his lie."

"Don't you think it possible he was embarrassed about knowing her?"

"Not him. He's more the bragging type."

"Come have some dessert and settle down. It's cherry cheesecake. I have something to discuss with you." She led me to a table where Heath and Mom were already eating their cake. "I want to tell all of you at the same time."

"Oh, gracious, you're getting married." Mom tossed down her fork.

"Not anytime soon, sweetie." Grandma handed me a plate with a slice of cake. "Hush and let me talk. It might have some bearing on this case. When I'm finished, we'll decide whether I should tell Teddy or whether it's my imagination."

Grandma might be a bit flighty and lacking common sense in her wardrobe style, but I sincerely doubted she was imagining anything. She had my full attention.

"Are y'all ready?"

"Get on with it, mother." My mom crossed her arms. "You always have to be so dramatic."

"You're always droll."

"Ladies," Heath said. "Ida, please continue."

She leaned over the table. "I think someone here is after the old women's money."

"What makes you think that?" Heath cocked his head.

"Because I got a letter." She pulled a flier from her cavernous bag. This one was fluorescent pink and looked big enough to swallow my car. "It's inviting, women only, to an exciting career opportunity and states the woman must be over the age of sixty. Now...the only women over sixty who might indulge in a career opportunity are old rich broads. The perfect target for a scam artist."

I hated to admit it, but I agreed with her. "Are you going to go?"

"I thought it wise to attend out of curiosity and to see whether anything illegal was going on. Sue Ellen, you're coming with me."

"When is it?"

Grandma glanced at her watch. "In an hour. We'll just make it."

"Not exactly how I wanted to spend my evening."

"All you do is watch television. Come on. Shelby, I'll knock on your door when we're back."

Then, they breezed out the door. I glanced at Heath and invited him over for coffee while we waited.

We had just finished watching some shoot up bang bang action flick. with me covering my face with a pillow most of the time, when Grandma and Mom waltzed through the front door.

"I know who our killer is," Grandma announced with a grin. "Or at least one of two people."

Mom flopped into a chair. "That was the longest, most stressful two hours of my life. I had to pretend to be rich."

"Well, you do have a sizeable bank account," I reminded her. "Who is it?"

"Alan Barker and Damon Markson are promising that women will double their finances if they invest in their get-rich scheme." Grandma perched on the edge of the coffee table.

"What's the scheme?" I guessed I'd have to draw every little bit of information from her.

"Condos. They're supposedly building luxury condos along the Arkansas River." She studied her nails. "I doubt they are. I'm sure they'll take the money and run." She glanced up. "Should I tell Teddy."

"Yes." Heath pressed the button on

the remote to turn off the television. "Let him investigate this. You three are in the murders deep enough without adding something else."

"But what if they're related?" I thought it very possible. With this latest information, it seemed likely that Teresa's death had to do with money. "I think you should write them a dummy check and see what happens."

"I think you should tell Ted." Heath glared at me. "You gals have done a terrific job investigating this crime. Now, it's time to let the professionals handle it."

I gave him a quick kiss. "It's sweet that you worry about us."

"We can't help it, sweetheart," Grandma said. "As I've said before...it's a sickness with us."

"Not me." Mom glanced from one to the other. "I keep getting roped into coming along. I'd rather watch TV or read a book. Those won't get you killed."

"You don't need to get involved." I knew my mother was the most passive of us three.

She shook her head. "I'm the sane one. Who's going to keep the two of you in line if I'm not there?"

She did have a valid point.

"I'm calling Ted." Before any of us could stop her, Mom had dialed his number and told him to meet us at my cottage.

I swore I could hear him groan over the air waves.

"He's already on his way." Grandma smiled. "He spends most nights with me now."

"I do not want to hear this." Mom covered her ears. "Have you no shame? Shelby is sitting right there."

"She's a grown woman." Grandma rolled her eyes.

"With better morals than you, I

hope."

Actually, I did. While I found Grandma's antics humorous, I'd made a vow during Junior High church camp to save myself until marriage. Thank God, Donald ditched me at the altar. I much preferred Heath and his soft heart. He didn't treat me like a possession. He treated me like an equal. That was extremely sexy to me.

Fifteen minutes later, Ted barged in the door. "What now?" He planted a kiss on Grandma's forehead and speared me with a sharp glance.

"It's all her this time." I pointed at Grandma.

"It's true. I went to a seminar and discovered Alan Barker and Damon Markson are scamming old ladies out of their life savings. I'm going to write them a dummy check to trip them up."

"You are not." He planted his fists on his hips. "You might end up their next victim."

I straightened. "So, you do suspect one of them."

"Maybe." He avoided my gaze. "I still don't want any of you women involved."

Grandma and I exchanged a glance. We'd be trying to trap the men for sure. We just needed a surefire way of doing so.

"You're wasting your breath," Heath said. "The air is vibrating with secret messages going back and forth between these two. The best we can do is keep an eye on them."

"You do it. I'm trying to close this case."

"If you're deputizing him, then I want to be deputized, too." I raised my hand.

"Me, too!" Grandma bolted to her feet.

Ted shook his head. "I have no idea what the two of you are talking about. This isn't the wild wild west. Stay out of my investigation or I'll lock you up for your own protection." He kissed Grandma again, took her by the arm, and practically dragged her toward the door.

"I do love a tough man," she twittered over her shoulder.

I wanted to gag.

"Your grandmother is cute." Heath pulled me close. "Sue Ellen, I plan on kissing your daughter senseless, so you might want to disappear."

Mom sighed. "I'll be in the bathroom for three minutes and not a second more."

Heath laughed, pushed me back on the sofa, and proceeded to make the most of our three minutes. Those were the fastest minutes ever. When Mom cleared her throat, I opened my eyes and blinked like a baby owl, a bit unsure of where I was.

"Yep. Senseless," Mom said. She clamped her lips together, but not before

I saw the glimmer of a smile. "Say goodnight Heath," she told me.

"Goodnight, Heath."

"Now," Mom said, gathering her purse. "I'd like an escort home. It isn't safe out there. Shelby, lock your door. You don't want to wake up dead."

20

I didn't wake up dead the next morning, but I did wake up with a renewed purpose. I was going to dig into this scam Alan and Damon were a part of.

Lying in bed, I once again ran through what I knew. Which wasn't as much as I would like.

Hold the presses! My mind honed in on Teresa's stack of magazines. Where was Teresa's box of magazines? I hadn't thrown them out and they weren't sold at the yard sale. Maybe she had a purpose for holding on to them. A purpose other than trying to live as those inside the pages did.

I quickly got dressed and found Alice at breakfast. "Where is the box of Teresa's magazines?"

She rolled her eyes. "Don't tell me you're into that garbage."

"No, I want to check something. Do we still have them?"

"They're in a corner of my office. Feel free to toss them when you're finished."

I wasn't sure why, but I ducked into the bathroom to see whether I had another message. I did. This one said, "Look behind you."

Spiders ran up my spine. Instead of turning, I searched the stalls through the mirror. No feet were visible under the door. A voice inside my head screamed for me to run.

As I turned and lunged for the door, Lauren shot from one of the stalls. She shrieked and raised a hand clutching a knife.

"You ruined my life!" The force of her crashing into me knocked me to my back on the floor.

I wrapped both of my hands around her wrist and fought to keep the knife from plunging into my chest. "You're...insane."

Good. My words had the intended effect. She continued to cause an ear-splitting racket. Someone was bound to hear. I prayed it was soon. The woman was bigger and stronger than me. All I had over her was the determination not to die at her hands.

I arched my back, throwing her off me, then scrambled on my hands and knees for the door.

She clawed at my leg.

A well-aimed kick caught her in the nose.

Blood spurted.

"Help!" Using the doorknob, I pulled myself to my feet.

By now, Lauren had regained her footing and was charging me again.

I yanked open the door and we both fell into the short hallway. By now, we had the attention of everyone in the dining hall.

Heath came running and yanked Lauren off me. When she raised the knife again, he grabbed her arm, bending it behind her back until the knife fell to the floor.

"Someone find Ted!" He wrapped his arms around Lauren, keeping her arms pinned to her side.

Curses and spittle flew from her lips.

I sagged against the opposite wall wishing I had the energy to punch her. Now that Heath had rescued me, I was as weak as a newborn colt.

Ted arrived with handcuffs and relieved Heath of his screaming, kicking burden. "Lauren Westingham, you're under arrest for the attempted murder of Heath McLeroy and Shelby Hart." He proceeded to read her her rights as he dragged her from the building.

Heath took me in his arms. "It's all right. You're fine now."

"Where could she have been hiding to sneak into the bathroom every day?" I rested my forehead against his chest. Why hadn't she come for me at my cottage? There would have been less chance of anyone saving me. Still, the woman was insane, and there was no making sense of a person with a messed up mind.

Heath led me to a chair. "The only place she could have hid was the tunnels. There must be several exits."

"You sure know how to hook a girl."

He laughed, sitting next to me. "She's always shown signs of crazy. It's my handsome physique and overwhelming charm that set her over the edge."

"Careful. Your ego is inflating." I

glanced down the hall. "I'm not cleaning up the blood from her nose."

"I'll get the cleaning girls to do it."

"I was actually headed for Alice's office to retrieve the box of Teresa's magazines, when I decided to check the bathroom for another message. I didn't really expect to find one."

"I'll get them for you. You rest. When I get back, I'll get you some breakfast." He hurried to the manager's office.

I folded my arms on the table and laid my head down. That was a close call. Too close. If only Lauren had killed Teresa and Ms. Wilkinson the hunt would be over.

"This is heavy." Heath set the box on the chair next to me. "How many magazines did she have?"

"A lot. I want to see if there is something in them to give us a clue to her killer."

He raised an eyebrow. "In a

Hollywood gossip mag?"

"It's a feeling I have."

"All right. We can get your mother and grandmother to help. Between the four of us, we can flip through them in an hour or so after supper." He went to the buffet, returning with a ham and cheese omelet for me.

"Do you want me to take you home? I'm sure Alice will understand." Heath set a glass of iced tea next to my plate.

"I'm not hurt, and I really need to so some weeding in the vegetable garden. I'll be fine. If you could drop that box off at my cottage...put it in the oven. No one will look for it there." Better safe than sorry. If there was something in the magazines, the killer might try to steal them.

"I'm not going to ask why you want it there." He grinned.

I returned his smile, finished my breakfast, then collected my things from the garden shed. While I knelt beside the green onions, pulling out the vegetation that didn't belong, I kept looking over my shoulder. I knew Ted had Lauren locked up by now, but a killer still roamed. I almost expected a knife in my back while I worked. Not a pleasant way to spend the morning.

By lunch time, my nerves were strung tight. Rather than be social in the dining hall, I headed for my cottage and a granola bar with yogurt. I could skim a few magazines while I ate before planning the big event in the maze.

Once I'd finished eating, and wasted two much time reading two magazines rather than skimming them, I booted up my laptop and started work on the flier for Saturday's event.

I specified for everyone to dress comfortably and come at dark with a flashlight. First person to find the prize, wins it. Simple and straightforward. Now, to get Alice to approve.

I headed for her office where she sat pouring over financial statements. "May I come in?"

"Sure. I'm going cross-eyed looking at these things. Good thing is, we're making a profit." She beamed and leaned back in her chair. "All the cottages are full. My uncle booked the last one."

So, Ted had made the move. I wondered when he'd retire. That seemed the next logical choice. "Having a police officer close by will be handy."

"Especially with you around." She wiggled her fingers. "Is that the flier? Let me see it."

I handed it to her and waited.

"When you first mentioned this idea, I thought it great, now…it seems too dangerous with a killer on the loose."

"I agree, but I'm hoping this will draw the killer out. I'll be wandering the maze, alone." Scary, but ought to do the trick.

"I'll have my Tazor, and I'll have Ted put a wire on me."

"I don't think you should go alone, but it's your neck." She approved the flier and handed it back to me. "Get these distributed today, please."

That was my intention, but I held my tongue. Barking orders seemed to make Alice feel important. "Have you heard of the scam Alan and Damon are running?"

"No." She frowned. "I won't allow that kind of thing to go on here."

I sat in the nearest chair. "I think one of them, maybe both, are our killer or killers. They've contradicted themselves about knowing Teresa, and now they're trying to get women to turn over their life savings."

"If you get proof, let me know. I'll kick them out on the spot." She made a shooing motion with her hand.

Dismissed, I headed back outside. After a month of working at Shady Acres, the grounds looked very good, if I said so myself. Bushes were trimmed, summer flowers were blooming, and all I needed to do was get the riding lawnmower and take care of the larger grassy areas. Not a chore I minded.

By supper time, I was dirty, sweaty, and starving. After a quick shower, I joined my family in the dining hall. Rather than eat there, we loaded our plates and headed to my place to browse the magazines.

We each grabbed a stack. Soon, the only sound in the place was the clink of silverware against porcelain and the rustle of papers.

"I knew it!" Grandma held up a picture of a famous actress. "I knew she'd had a boob job and collagen in her butt. No one's behind is that big without a little help."

I scowled. "You're looking for news on people we actually know. Someone that could have killed Teresa."

"Rather a long shot," Mom said.

"Yes, it is, but the feeling that we'll find something here hasn't diminished all day."

"I need wine." Grandma jumped up and searched my cupboards. "Ah ha! You have a bottle."

"I keep one here just for you."

She kissed the top of my head. "That's my girl. Anyone else?"

We all shook our heads. I, for one, wanted a clear head in case I actually found something.

"I feel as if I'm getting dumber with each turn of the page." Heath tossed one back in the box and grabbed another.

"It doesn't hurt to stay up with social and cultural events," Grandma said, pouring her wine glass full. "It gives you something to talk about over dinner."

"I'd rather talk about the weather than this garbage."

"Hold up." Mom turned her magazine around. "Isn't this Alan Barker?"

We gathered around her. Sure enough, a small article on a YouTube tycoon suspected of stealing other people's material and posting as his own. The article was two years old.

I took the magazine from her. "If Teresa confronted him with this, he might have killed her."

"Don't jump to conclusions," Heath said. "But, it does look suspicious."

The lights went out, plunging us into darkness.

"I'll check the fuse box," Heath said. "Nobody move."

We sat in the dark, not speaking. Finally, Heath appeared. At least, I'd thought it was him until the magazine was ripped out of my hand and the shadowy figure yanked open the front door and dashed out.

"After him! He has the evidence." I

ran out.

"I'll get my gun!" Grandma followed, her pink pistol clutched in her hand.

"Stop!" Heath, holding a hand to his head, blocked our path. "He hit me over the head. You can't go chasing after him. Especially if Ida is armed. I'll go."

"Did you get a good look at him?" I asked.

"No. He was hiding in your closet, which is where the fuse box is. He had to have been listening to our conversation. Get back in the cottage and lock the door. Call Ted." He whirled and raced after the fleeing man.

Chasing the man was futile. He had too much of a head start.

I headed back inside, where Mom cowered under a floral blanket. I cast her a glance, then headed to my bedroom. Yep, the window was wide open. I hadn't left it that way when I'd gone that morning.

A closer look showed the window had been jimmied open. I used a couple of books to keep the window from opening all the way and sat down to wait for Ted.

21

*H*eath and Ted arrived back at my place together.

"You found what in a gossip rag?" Ted said, his brow furrowed.

"Do listen up, dear. It takes too long to repeat ourselves." Grandma patted his arm before retrieving her wine and putting her gun back in her purse.

"Who gave Ida a gun?" His voice rose.

"No one, sweetie. I purchased it myself. I could have got that scoundrel if Heath hadn't gotten in the way." She pouted, then turned her attention to the glass in her hand.

"He broke my window getting in," I said.

"I'll fix it." Heath headed immediately for my room.

Having a handy man for a boyfriend came in handy. "Now, what?" I glanced up at Ted.

"This is one slippery devil." Ted sat on the arm of Grandma's chair. "The only thing we know for sure is it's a male and he probably lives at Shady Acres."

"We know that it's Alan Barker." Grandma raised her glass.

"We can't prove it. All we have is circumstantial evidence."

I was going to catch the culprit on Saturday. I knew it. I only prayed I'd live through the capture.

"I heard you rented Teresa's cottage," I said to Ted. "Retiring soon?"

"Maybe." He smiled down at Grandma. "I'm thinking it's time to take things a little slower. Chasing bad guys should be left to the younger men."

"What will you do with your time?" Grandma drained her glass. "I know. You can help keep Shelby out of trouble."

He laughed and shook his head. "An impossible task for one man. She needs a SWAT team."

"Very funny."

"Window is fixed. I put a new lock on it. No one is getting in without you letting them in."

"Thank you. Now, if you all don't mind, I'm going to bed." I kissed Heath good night, told them to lock the door behind themselves, and then slid under my covers.

I'd had solid evidence in my hand and, literally, let it get snatched away. I knew Alan was the killer, well, him or Damon, Ted knew it, but we needed a taped confession practically. "Ted!"

Mom came to my room. "You cannot yell for a man to come to your bedroom."

"Fine. Tell him I want one of those little recording devices."

"I heard her!"

"He heard you."

"I'll leave it on the kitchen table!"

"He'll leave it on—"

"The cottage isn't that big, Mom."

Her cheeks darkened. "Right. Well, good night, then. Love you."

Soon, my cottage was quiet. Still sleep eluded me. Every time I closed my eyes I saw myself being chased by Lauren, who had blood pouring from her nose and a knife in her hand, and a man in a black hoodie.

I must have slept at some point, because I missed seeing the clock turn from one a.m. to six. With a groan, I got out of bed and headed for the shower.

I went to breakfast feeling as if I'd been beaten up. My eyes were full of sand. Maybe I should go back to bed and take a sick day.

"You look awful," Alice said the moment I entered the room.

"Gee, thanks. I think I'm sick."

"Don't even think about taking the day off. I need you here. Besides, if you were that sick, you would've stayed in bed in the first place."

"Would it have worked?"

"Yes." Alice handed me a stack of folders. "Distribute these to all the cottages. They're the new rules."

"Why do we need new rules?" This would take me all day!

"Because we have unsavory characters living here."

Did she really say unsavory characters? Who talked like that? "I don't think those type of people care much for rules."

"Just pass them out, please. I worked hard on them."

Fine. I now had the perfect excuse to

do more snooping. Add in the credit card sized recorder in my pocket and I was good to go. I needed coffee.

I set the folders on a nearby table and poured myself a half coffee, half hot chocolate, added whipped cream from a can and attempted to carry the whole kit and caboodle outside. Since none of my family had arrived, I thought it nice to enjoy my breakfast by the pool.

It was a good idea in theory. As I pushed open the door with my arms full of blue colored folders, the pile began to slip, the coffee spilled, and now I and the things I was supposed to distribute sported faded brown splotches. Alice was going to kill me.

"For crying out loud." Alice seemed to appear out of nowhere, took the soiled packets, and handed me a stack of new ones. "For some reason, I knew something would happen to the first stack. Where are you going?"

"To the pool," I mumbled.

"I'll bring you another cup of coffee."

I shouted out how I enjoyed my chocolate coffee and took the packets to one of the poolside tables. I might as well read the rules myself before weeks passed and someone called me on it.

It was a good thing there was nothing in my mouth, because I would have spewed it out at rule number one. "No killing of other residents. This is mandatory."

I snickered and continued reading. Rule number two, "No stealing of other people's things." She might as well have listed the ten commandments, but her way was more entertaining.

"Are you laughing at the rules?" She plopped my coffee on the table, spilling some, and propped her hands on her hips.

"I'm trying not to. Seriously, Alice...no charging for sexual favors?"

She sat across from me. "I'm trying to clean the place up. I've never worked at a more stressful place. None of my past jobs were a danger to my life." She glared at me as if I were the cause.

"You do know Maybelle would have died if you hadn't hired me, right?" I sipped my coffee. "It's good. What did you add?"

"Cinnamon." She sighed. "Yes, I know her death was a coincidence with your arrival and that you aren't responsible for how Teresa chose to live her life. She seemed like such a nice girl."

"She *was* a nice girl. Just misguided." I took another sip of the coffee and wished I'd thought of cinnamon.

"My life is nothing like I thought it would be by the age of thirty. Today is my birthday. I'm unmarried, childless, no boyfriend, and a job that consumes my every waking minute."

"Happy Birthday. Why didn't you tell

anyone?"

"I don't like a fuss. It's just another day. I promised Uncle Ted to secrecy." She glanced around the pool area, empty except for the two of us. "This is nice. I should come out here more often when the weather is right. Very relaxing."

"You can always work out at the gym when it's complete."

"That won't be for a few more weeks. But, that is a good idea." She stood and strolled away, reminding me again not to fail in delivering the folders and not to ruin these because she didn't have anymore.

Gee, just when we'd had a moment together she reverts back to her bossy self.

I finished my coffee, returned the cup to the dining hall, then started delivering the folders. At most people's cottages, I left the folders on the mat in front of their door. At Damon's I knocked.

"Well, if it isn't the lovely…what's on your shirt?"

"Coffee."

"Why didn't you change before someone saw you?" He leaned against the doorjamb. "I mean, wearing rain boots and faded denim is one thing when you're working, but when you're socializing, a woman should look her best."

For crying out loud. "It happened on my way over here. I'm sorry if I offend you." I thrust out the rules. "Here."

He took the folder and shook his head. The man actually looked sad. "I'd had high hopes for us, Shelby. But a woman who can't keep up her appearance has no place in my life."

"Is that what happened to Teresa? You had no more use for her so you killed her?" I backed up two steps.

"That nosiness of yours is going to get you into trouble." He lunged forward, grabbed my arm, and shook me like a rag in a dog's mouth. "Let it go!"

I yanked free. "She deserves justice and I aim to see she gets it." Darn. I'd forgotten to turn on the tape recorder. I stuck my hand in my pocket and pressed the button.

"I'm going to find her killer, Damon."

"Then you'll end up the same way." He stepped back and slammed the door.

I knocked again.

"What?" He yanked it open.

"I know about your scam and won't let my mother, or grandmother, have any part of it." I switched off the recorder and sauntered away. Not exactly a confession, but it might give Ted something to work with.

I did the same thing at Alan's. Knocked, stepped back, but this time I turned on the recorder the moment he opened the door. "What?"

He definitely didn't have the charm

his friend did. "New resident rules."

He took the folder and tossed it behind him into the house.

I had a better look at the scratches on his neck. They were healing, but looked suspiciously like fingernail scratches to me. "What happened?" I pointed.

"An irate girlfriend."

"I didn't know you were dating anyone."

"Contrary to what you seem to think, my personal life is none of your business. Move along, little girl."

"Excuse me? There's no need to be rude." I straightened as tall as my five foot two inch frame would allow. "Why did you pretend not to know Teresa when in all actuality, you knew her very well?"

"Again, none of your business." He tried to close the door.

I stuck my foot in the way. "Did she make you mad? Did she find the article against you in one of her magazines?"

While his face paled, high spots of color rose on his cheeks. "Back off."

"Or what? Will you kill me the same way you killed her? I doubt you'll leave me flowers, though. A pity, really. Every girl likes flowers from her man." I grinned. "Not that you're my man. You aren't my type. Have a good day, Mr. Barker."

I paused and turned for dramatic effect. "I know about the scam. Stay away from my family."

I strolled away, my heart in my throat. I'd seen the missing magazine on his coffee table and knew I'd awoken a sleeping beast.

Making short order of dropping off the rest of the files, I headed to the maze. I wanted to make a banner for the entrance and string twinkling lights to add a festive air. Inside the maze, there would be fog, scary noises, etc. Anything

I could think of to make the adventure more thrilling.

"Boo." Heath wrapped his arounds around my waist from the back and lifted me off my feet. "What have you been up to?"

I told him and then let him listen to the recordings.

A muscle ticked in his jaw. "I wish you wouldn't have gone alone, much less provoked them."

"I was doing my job." Except, I'd done a bit more and increased the target on my back.

"I wish you didn't have this desire for justice."

"You don't?" Surprise laced my words.

"That didn't come out right. Of course, I believe everyone deserves justice. I wish you weren't the one trying to get it. Let the authorities handle things."

He sounded like a broken record.

"You were singing a different tune when you were a suspect."

"Yes, and I appreciate your help clearing my name." He gazed at me, his face creased with worry. "That was before I fell in love with you, Shelby. I can't protect my girl if she does dangerous things without me."

"You love me?"

"Yes, God help me, I do." He pulled me close and gave me a warm kiss. "But, it's a part of you, and I'll do my best to adjust."

I cupped his face. "Thank you." I wanted to tell him I loved him, too, but fear held me back. I knew he wasn't like Donald. Not at all. But, still...someday, maybe, I could freely give my heart again.

22

Alan and Damon glared at me the moment I walked into the dining room the next morning. I smiled and waved, certain I had struck a nerve that would push the killer to show himself.

The mood around my table was subdued. From the glowering glances Ted sent my way, Heath must have told him about the recordings.

"Here." Rather than wait for him to order me to hand them over, I did so on my own accord.

"No wonder your mother is as skittish as a rabbit." He stuck the recording in his pocket. "You're a parent's nightmare."

"I'm skittish?" The bacon headed to Mom's mouth paused as she frowned.

He nodded. "Skittish. But, you're also the most level headed woman in your family."

That seemed to appease her, and she continued eating. "You're right," she said. "No telling where these two would be if I didn't keep an eye on them."

Grandma and I shared an amused glance.

"If not for me," Grandma said, "Sue Ellen would be even more of a fuddy duddy than she already is. Lord knows I've tried to show her how to have fun."

"Putting your life in danger is not my idea of fun." Mom scowled. "Besides, I do have fun. I enjoy my life. Leave me alone."

"I'm going to wear a wire on Saturday," I informed Ted. "I'm certain the killer will take that opportunity to show himself to me."

"I'll be stalking her every move," Heath said, setting his glass of orange juice down with a definitive thump. "I'll stay out of your sight, but you will be in mine every second."

"And mine." Ted crossed his arms. "I think this maze in the dark while there is a killer loose is stupid and irresponsible, but you're right. He'll most likely make his move, and I don't like it one bit. You shouldn't be the bait."

"Feel free to take my place." Somehow I didn't think it would have the same effect. "I'll have my Tazor, a commercial size flashlight, and you two dogging my every move. Unless the killer has a sniper rifle, which doesn't seem to be their method of choice, I'll be fine. I have to be in the maze. My purpose is to show those who are lost the way."

"Will you be as fine as when Lauren attacked you in the restroom?" Heath raised his eyebrows.

"I was fighting her off." I was losing the battle, but I was still fighting.

"Yeah, it looked like it." He transferred his attention to the plate in front of him.

Unusually surly, led me to believe his feelings were hurt because I hadn't returned his declaration of love the night before. When things settled down, I'd do my best to explain. Until then, I'd continue on as we were. If he truly loved me, he wouldn't walk away just yet.

After breakfast, I went to remove the magazines from my cottage. On the way to the recycling bin, I heard men's voices coming from the area behind the pool where the pump was located.

I ducked and listened, pretty sure it was Alan and Damon. I pressed record on the device in my pocket.

"We need to shut her up," Alan said. "I need the money from these old ladies.

With Teresa gone...well, my new woman is costing me an arm and a leg."

"I've warned you about high priced women," Damon said. "Do you have any ideas on how to continue? That nosy Shelby is smarter than the girls we're used to. I've tried disarming her with my charm, but she doesn't go for it. She's faithful to the handyman."

"Too bad. If you remove the handyman from the equation, you could swoop in and get her while she's vulnerable. If she's with you, she won't be a problem."

"True. She isn't the type to fool around like Teresa."

I was no longer the target. Heath was! I needed to alert him. Making enough noise to alert them to the fact someone was close by, I banged open the dumpster lid and tossed the magazines in. Only then did I realize that if they looked in the dumpster, they'd know I was the one who had had all the magazines.

I groaned. Idiot. Maybe they wouldn't look.

Quick walking, okay, jogging, away from the pool, I went in search of Heath. I found him scooping dead leaves from the koi pond.

"You need to hear this." I handed him the recording.

After listening, his face impassive, he said, "Good. Better me than you."

"No!" I gripped his arm. "I'm prepared for them, you aren't."

He shook free. "I'm better able to protect myself than you are. Besides, Ted will be close by."

How was I supposed to concentrate during Saturday's event if I worried about Heath? Now, instead of patrolling the maze, I'd be following him around. "You don't understand."

"No, it's you who doesn't

understand." He sat on the brick wall surrounding the pond. "I'll rest easier knowing you aren't the target."

"I won't rest at all knowing you are!"

He shrugged one shoulder. "I guess we're at a stale mate."

"I guess we are." Tears clogged my throat. "I don't want the people I care about in danger."

"You can't have it all, Shelby." He exhaled sharply. "At least you admit to caring about me."

"You know I do. Don't do this. We'll talk after Saturday."

"Fine." He stood. "Now, if you'll excuse me, I have work to do." He turned his back.

I blinked, trying to hold the tears at bay. Our first real argument and I wasn't sure our relationship would survive.

"Shelby!" Alice clunked on her stilettos toward me.

I sniffed and wiped my eyes. "Yeah?"

She narrowed her eyes. "Are you crying?"

"Allergies."

"Oh, yeah, they're tough this time of year. I have an idea for Saturday. Walk with me to the kitchen."

I'd never been in the kitchen before. At any other time, excitement might have peppered my steps. Today, I dragged.

"My idea is to have some kind of mystery food for Saturday's dinner. But, I'm drawing a blank."

Was she serious? Who wanted to eat something they didn't know what it was? I thought for a moment, then had an idea. "How about making up different ethnic meals and putting them in plain dinner boxes? No one will know what they're getting at first, but they'll recognize the food once they open the box."

"Great idea." She grinned. "That's

why I hired you. Now, run out and get me sixty of those type boxes." Handing me a credit card, she shooed me from the kitchen before I had both feet in the room.

I texted Grandma to see if she wanted to go with me. She did. A few minutes later, we were both in my little Volkswagon and headed for the nearest warehouse store.

"I never turn down a chance to stock up on my wine," Grandma said.

"Your liver ought to be quite pickled by now."

"Everyone knows it's the hard stuff that hurts your liquor. Wine is good for you."

Whatever she said. An hour later, the backseat filled with wine bottles, boxes, and clothes Grandma just had to have, we headed home.

As I drove, I asked her advice regarding Heath.

"Why didn't you say the words back?" She tilted her head, looking just like a wrinkled puppy.

"I'm afraid."

"Oh, pooh. I didn't raise a coward."

She didn't raise me at all. In fact, until I graduated high school, I rarely knew my world-traveling grandmother.

"I've told Teddy dozens of times. Love is cheap, dearie, commitment is what costs you. It's clear you love the man, so say the words. Take a chance. He isn't your ex."

While I thought her reasoning regarding love a bit skewed, she did make a valid point. "I'll tell him after tomorrow night's event." I glanced in my rearview mirror as a dark truck with tinted windows rode on my bumper.

I pulled to the slow lane so they could pass. Instead of increasing their speed, they slowed and hit the side of my car. "Hey!" Not my baby. "I thought Heath was the target now."

"Perhaps you both are." Grandma dug her fingernails into the dashboard. "Can you outrun them?"

"In this bug? Not a chance." I stopped and threw the car into reverse.

The truck did the same.

A curve up ahead sent a bolt of fear through me. If I couldn't avoid them before we reached it...I turned the wheel and sped back the way we'd come.

"I'm calling Teddy!" Grandma fished her phone from her purse.

I didn't know what he could do, but it wouldn't hurt to let someone know what was happening. I pressed the accelerator and pushed my baby to her limit.

It didn't take long for the truck to be on my bumper again. "What do I do?"

"Take a defensive driving class as soon as possible. Teddy? We're being run off the road...yes, Shelby is driving...Ted says to get off the road as soon as possible."

"Where?" Trees lined the highway.

The truck rammed us from behind.

"Oh, that hit clicked my teeth together. I almost bit my tongue, Teddy..." she smiled. "He said he'll kiss it later."

Gross. "Hush and let me concentrate." I whipped the wheel again, taking us toward the truck.

"Oh, good Lord, she's playing chicken with the truck!"

"I am not." I'd spotted a dirt road off to the side. Before the truck could turn, I'd pulled in and drove behind some bushes. "Tell Teddy we're at mile marker 102, down a dirt road. And hurry. It won't take long for them to find us."

"He said the tracker on your phone told him where we were and help is on the way."

"I forgot about that particular invasion of privacy." For once, I was glad to have the tracker on my phone.

Sirens wailed in the distance. Soon, a squad car pulled alongside us.

"Did you see them?"

The young officer shook his head, his eyes covered by mirrored sunglasses. "Nope. They must have left when they heard me coming. I'll follow you to your destination."

"How's my car?"

He glanced up and down. "A few scratches. A dent. Nothing that can't be fixed. It looks as if the assailant wanted to warn rather than harm. More importantly, are either one of you hurt?"

"My tongue is throbbing."

He pressed his lips together. "Let's go."

"You can be so embarrassing, Grandma." I pulled out of our hiding place. True to his word, the officer followed until I drove into the parking lot of Shady Acres.

That was a close call. One I didn't want to repeat any time soon.

Ted and Heath ran toward us as we got out of the car. While Ted grabbed Grandma in a hug, Heath wrapped his arms around me.

"I'm sorry. Let's not fight. What if an argument is the last thing we did?"

I tilted my face to his. "You aren't angry with me anymore?"

"I was never angry with you, only hurt. I've put my big boy pants on." He gave me a crooked grin. "Why is there something red dripping from the inside of your car?"

"My wine!" Grandma stomped her foot. "I demand retribution. That stuff isn't cheap."

Heath slid his arm around my waist and planted a kiss on my neck. "I'm glad you're okay."

"Let's do the maze together tomorrow." I glanced up. "It will be safer, and if something happens...which I'll pray it won't...there's no one I'd rather be in trouble with than you."

23

*H*eath squeezed my hand. "Ready?"

I nodded and watched as almost everyone from the community traipsed down the flagstone path to the maze. I clapped my hands to get their attention. "The fliers explained the rules, but I'll say them again. First one to find the prize, gets the prize. That's pretty much it. Heath and I will be wandering the maze with you in case you get hopelessly lost. Ready, set...go!"

Like a herd of thundering cattle they entered the maze. Alan and Damon were right in the thick of the crowd. Good. I'd almost thought they wouldn't show.

I glared at them as they passed, but both men avoided my gaze. Cowards. I glanced at Heath. "Ready?"

"Do you have your wire and Tazor?"

I nodded. "And my heavy flashlight."

"Don't get separated." He led me by the hand into the maze.

Clouds flirted with the moon, casting the maze into dark shadows. Perfect for the event.

The residents had also enjoyed the surprise dinner boxes and wanted them more often. I really was made for this job. I'd been a good teacher, but this...working with the gardens and seeing people smile at the activities I planned...was very fulfilling. Maybe someday I'd return to shaping little minds, but not any time soon.

The night filled with excited chatter until someone called out that talking alerted others to where you were and if you didn't shut up someone might beat you to the prize. Then, silence fell like a shooting star except for the giggles rising from my throat.

"I really do love these people," I said.

"All of them?" Heath's eyes sparkled.

"Most of them." I returned his smile and flicked on my flashlight. "Should we start moving or wait until someone calls for help?"

"Let's walk. Nothing like a moonlight stroll with my best girl. Besides, if we keep moving, it'll be harder to find us."

"Wait." I tugged him to a stop. "Finding us is the whole point."

"You do have the two-way wire on, right?"

I nodded. Ted had given it to me earlier that evening.

"Ow!" A cry sounded behind us.

We turned.

Alice sat on the ground rubbing her ankle. One of her ridiculous high heeled shoes lay beside her.

Heath rushed to her side. "You should know better than to wear heels in the maze."

"Help me to that bench. I've twisted it bad."

Another cry for help rang out.

I glanced at Heath, who was clearly torn between helping Alice and going with me. When Alice clutched his arm, I whirled and dashed away. Better I leave him safely behind.

I ran this way and that trying to determine where the call for help had come from. "Where are you?"

The cry came again.

I turned right and came to a dead end. Grinning at me were Alan and Damon.

"Look at that. She found us." Alan pulled a gun from his pocket.

"Whoa." Damon stepped in front of him. "What are you doing? We don't kill for the money. We're only here to scare her."

"You've served your purpose...friend." Alan pulled the trigger.

Damon dropped to the ground.

I rushed to his side and fell to my knees. "He's still alive. We need to get help."

"I'm afraid that isn't possible. Let's go." He waved the gun.

"Go where? There's only one way out."

"That's what you know. Head to the gazebo. Avoid Ted and Heath at all costs. You'd better hurry. If someone gets there before us, there may be more shots fired."

"You're insane."

"No, just desperate, and desperate people are dangerous." He shoved me. "Go."

I slipped my hand into my pocket and turned on the recorder. "I knew you were the killer."

"I figured as much. Women shouldn't be as smart as you. Now, stop talking before someone hears and follows us."

That's what I wanted. But, after too many jabs in the back with the gun, I took him to the gazebo. No one had found the prize yet. The box sat on the small table in the center.

"Move that table. There's a trapdoor under it. Hurry up." Alan jabbed me again.

Now I knew how Lauren got in and out to leave me messages. I moved the table and pulled up a door I hadn't known was there. You would have thought the workmen would have mentioned it. Instead, they'd repaired the door and gazebo as if it were perfectly natural to have a trapdoor.

I shined my flashlight down a set of wooden steps and took a deep breath. Here went nothing. I really hoped Ted was close enough to be following us.

"Turn right at the T-junction." Alan ordered.

"Where are we going?"

"Somewhere you can't find your way out until I'm long gone."

I stopped and turned, shining the light in his eyes. "You aren't going to kill me?"

"No, I'll let the dark do that." He sneered, slapping my hand down. "Don't blind me like that."

"May I ask why you killed Teresa?"

"You know why. She was blackmailing me with that stupid article."

"And Ms. Wilkinson?"

He shrugged. "I'm not positive she knew anything, but I couldn't take any chances. As for Damon, well, we had some laughs, but the man was too soft where women were concerned. He'd become a liability."

I stared at the heartless man in front of me, then brought the flashlight back up. I shined the beam directly into his eyes, then lashed out with the flashlight, clipping him on the side of the head. As he fell to his knees, I ran.

"I know these tunnels, sweetheart, and you don't."

True, but I wasn't going to make anything easy for him. I'd read somewhere that if you were lost, to always stay to the right. I ran deeper into the tunnels.

A shot rang out, then a curse.

My flashlight jerked in my hand, then sputtered out. The bullet must have clipped the light. Better the light, than me. Problem was...I was now cast into total darkness.

I trailed one hand down the wall and continued, watching for the small beam from Alan's light. He could no longer see me, but I could see him. All I needed to do was find a place to hide then zap him with my Tazor when he got close.

I tripped and fell. As I felt for the wall to get back up, my hand disappeared into an alcove. The perfect hiding place. I crawled inside and waited.

Darkness engulfed me. The odor of moist dirt filled my nostrils.

What if Ted didn't come? What if he really did leave me down here? The infernal tears that were never far behind when I was upset or scared sprang to the surface. No. I swiped them away. If he left, I'd find my way out. It might take a while, but I refused to die down there.

From somewhere came more cursing. It was hard to tell if he was coming my way or not.

With eyes wide open, I waited for a glimmer of light to signal he was close.

"I changed my mind. I am going to kill you! Slowly!"

I shuddered. "Ted? If you can hear me, I'm in the tunnels. Alan is coming, and he's mad. Hurry," I whispered.

"Sit tight and be quiet," Ted's voice came over the piece in my ear. "I'm on my way."

"Please, hurry." I scooted as far back as I could.

A faint light broke through the darkness. I got my Tazor ready.

Alan stopped in front of my hiding place. "I smell the perfume you're wearing."

"It's body spray." I reached out and zapped his ankle.

He shrieked and fell.

I scrambled for the flashlight and the gun, tripping over his body. The flashlight slammed into the wall and went out. Okay. I'd try to be positive. I was stuck in the dark, with a killer, but I had the gun and a Tazor. My phone!

I pulled it from my pocket and shined the light on Alan's face. His eyes glittered with evil intent. I zapped him again, then kicked him for good measure.

"Shelby!" Ted yelled in my ear.

"That hurt. Speak softly, please."

"What's going on? Where are you?"

"In the tunnels. I fought Alan and won. He's twitching like a fish on a line right now. I have enough juice in my Tazor for one more zap so you'd better hurry. Oh, and call out before you run up on me. I'm sitting in the dark with a gun. I'd hate to shoot you."

He chuckled. "I'd hate that, too."

I shut off the light on my phone. I'd use it again when Alan stirred, which would be in about twenty more seconds. I wasn't out of trouble yet.

"I suppose I could shoot you in the leg and leave you for the rats, but, you see, Alan...I'm a nicer person that that." I hit him with the flashlight in the head, then flashed my phone long enough to see I'd knocked him out. "That's what people get when they try to kill me.

"I would say it wasn't personal, but it

kind of is. I need you to stay unconscious until help arrives." I slid my back up the wall until I stood on my feet.

I turned and glanced down the tunnel. Where was Ted?

Arms grabbed me and swung me off my feet.

I kicked as hard as I could, connecting with Alan's shin.

"Give me the gun!"

"No." I tossed it into the dark. Now, neither one of us could see.

He released me and grappled for my throat.

I stepped back, willing my breath to be slow and easy. He huffed so loud it had to be hard to hear me.

"I am going to squeeze the life out of you!"

He had to find me first. Inch-by-inch I moved backward. I stepped on something.

My ankle twisted.

I fell.

Wait. It was the gun.

I crawled on the dirt floor looking for it.

A light shined in my face. I blinked against the glare.

Alan had the same thought of using his cell phone. He bent and retrieved the gun at his feet. "Get up."

His tone made my blood run cold.

"What's wrong? Don't you like your women feisty?"

"I said. Get. Up."

Fine. He was in no mood for games. I stood and squared my shoulders. If he was going to shoot me, I was going to take it like a soldier. I closed my eyes.

Please, don't hurt. Please, don't hurt. Oh, I'd heard getting shot hurt bad.

"What are you mumbling?"

My eyes popped open. "Prayers."

"Good grief. Stand against the wall."

So, it was to be execution style. Be

brave, Shelby.

He cursed and pulled the trigger.

The bullet caught me in the thigh.

I screamed and fell as pain ripped through my leg.

"Ciao, baby." He whirled and ran.

Another shot rang out.

I heard a muffled thump, then someone shined a light in my eyes.

"Shelby!" Heath swooped me into his arms. "She's hit." Without waiting for anyone else, he dashed back the way he'd come. The path was lit by the lantern on the helmet he wore.

"I'm glad to see you," I said.

"Shh. Don't talk."

My leg throbbed with every jar of his running. "You're hurting me, Heath. Slow down."

"I can't. You might die." He kept running.

"I'm shot in the leg, not the heart." I wrapped my arms around his neck.

"I'm sorry." He slowed. "When I heard the gun go off…"

"Where's Ted?"

"Checking out the body."

"So, Alan is dead?"

"Very much so. Ted is a good shot." He slowed even more, his breathing growing labored. "For a little thing, you get heavy."

I sighed and rested my head against his chest. His heart beat a steady, but fast, rhythm against my cheek. He was alive. I was still breathing. All was right in my world again.

24

I opened my eyes to the sound of beeping hospital machines and the odor of disinfectant. My leg throbbed and my throat ached for a drink of water.

"Here." Mom appeared as if by magic with a small plastic cup and bendy straw. "How are you feeling?"

"Sore." It all came rushing back. The dark. The tunnel. The bullet tearing through my thigh. "How bad was it?"

"Went clean through. No surgery required." Mom smiled. "It could have been worse, Shelby. I hope you reconsider before getting involved in another murder." She sat in the mint green vinyl chair beside my bed.

"I will definitely consider it." I grinned and relaxed against my pillows. I'd done it again. Taken down a killer. With help, of course, but once again justice was served. "Where's Heath?"

"Getting coffee. This is the first time he's left your side since you were brought in yesterday." Her eyes glimmered with tears. "You scared me half to death, Shelby."

I reached over and took her hand. "I'm sorry."

"Why can't you be normal?"

"Because she's too much like me." Grandma breezed into the room, followed by Ted. "We live life to the fullest. Nothing keeps us down. Good morning, darling." She kissed my cheek.

I smiled at her, but my gaze met Ted's. "Thank you."

He nodded. "You're a lucky girl,

Shelby Hart."

"It could have ended differently if you hadn't found me."

He chuckled. "You managed to do quite the number on Alan Barker. The man was bleeding from a head wound and had Tazor burns on his ankle before I arrived."

That's what happens when you're fighting for your life. I peered around him, my heart leaping at the sight of Heath standing in the doorway.

"Everyone out," he said. "I plan on kissing my girl."

My face heated to match the burn in my leg.

The other three skedaddled. Grandma winked before closing the door.

"We'd better hurry," I said. "The nurses will wonder why the door is closed."

He set the coffee on a side table, then

bent over me, resting his forehead against mine. "I thought I'd lost you."

"Takes more than a little bullet in the leg to stop me." Oh, I would have a scar. I sighed. My skinny legs were more flawed than ever. "Kiss me until I forget yesterday."

He was more than happy to oblige. We kissed, him stretched out by my side, until the nurse came in.

"Careful of the leg," she said. "How's the patient? The pain level?"

"What pain," I giggled, running my finger over my swollen lips.

She laughed. "If this man's kisses takes away the pain, we should bottle him. We'd make a fortune."

I caressed Heath's face. "Sorry, but I'm not sharing."

The nurse took my vitals, then left as the others returned. Heath sighed and slid from the bed.

"Okay, Ted, tell me what happened?"

I sat up.

"Well, Damon told us—"

"He's alive?"

Ted nodded. "The scam was real. They'd made a lot of money off unsuspecting women. The bullet caught him in the ribs, breaking one, but he'll survive. Alan, not so much." He sat in the empty chair. "My shot took care of him. He'd made a fortune stealing other people's Youtube material and passing it off as his own. When Teresa discovered what he'd done, she tried to blackmail him. At least, that's the best we can figure out."

"It's always about money." I sighed.

"Money is the root of all evil," Grandma said. "That's in the Bible."

"No, it isn't. The love of money is what it says." Same thing, sort of. Oh, the pain meds were starting to make me drowsy and light headed. "When can I go home?"

"The doctor will be in soon to sign the release papers." Ted patted my good leg. "It's good to still have you around, kid. Stay away from killers."

"Now, Teddy, you know she can't promise that." Grandma's eyes widened. "Trouble follows her like a kid with a dollar chases an ice cream truck. She'll be headfirst in trouble within a month. I guarantee it."

Especially with Grandma helping me. Maybe solving crime, unofficially of course, helped her feel young. Either way, it gave me a thrill I never thought to experience. Now, if I could get justice for those who can't get it themselves, without my life being in danger...that would be the cream on top of a brownie. "I'm hungry."

"We'll grab a cheeseburger as soon as you're free from here." Heath raised my hand and kissed it. "I plan on taking care of you twenty-four seven."

"Oh, no, you don't." Mom crossed her arms. "I'll be staying in her cottage until she can manage on her own."

Heath laughed. "I love getting your mother riled."

"She riles easily," I whispered.

"I can hear you. I'm standing right here." Mom huffed and left the room.

Grandma watched her go. "I have no idea where I went wrong with that girl. She needs a man. That is going to be my goal."

"Oh, no." I laughed, the action jarring my leg. Still, I couldn't stop laughing even through the pain. "I'd better warn her."

"Hush."

I loved my life. Surrounded by the people I loved, a job I enjoyed, a romance to keep things spicy, and a touch of danger now and then to keep me on my toes, what could be better.

I grabbed Heath's hand and pulled his ear close to my lips. "I love you."

He grinned. "It's about time."

"Can you handle another adventure with me?" I had no doubt something would come along.

"Sure, but let's get you healed first, all right?"

"Agreed." I pulled him down for another kiss.

The End

Stay tuned for the next Shady Acres mystery

ABOUT THE AUTHOR

Multi-published and Amazon Best-Selling author Cynthia Hickey had three cozy mysteries and two novellas published through Barbour Publishing. Her first mystery, Fudge-Laced Felonies, won first place in the inspirational category of the Great Expectations contest in 2007. Her third cozy, Chocolate-Covered Crime, received a four-star review from Romantic Times. All three cozies have been re-released as ebooks through the MacGregor Literary Agency, along with a new cozy series, all of which stay in the top 50 of Amazon's ebooks for their genre. She had several historical romances release in 2013, 2014, 2015 through Harlequin's Heartsong Presents, and has sold half a million copies of her works. She has taught a Continuing Education class at the 2015 American Christian Fiction Writers conference. She is active on FB, twitter, and Goodreads, and is a contributor to Cozy Mystery Magazine blog and Suspense Sisters blog. She and her husband run the small press, Forget Me Not Romances, which includes some of the CBA's well-known authors. She lives in Arizona with her husband, one of their seven children, two dogs, two cats, three box turtles, and two Sulcata tortoises. She has seven grandchildren who keep her busy and tell everyone they know that "Nana is a writer". Visit her website at www.cynthiahickey.com

Made in United States
Troutdale, OR
06/30/2023

10895424R00207